and the Intergalactic Zoo

Poog

Gax

Akiko

Mr. Beeba

Spuckler

and the Intergalactic Zoo

Written and illustrated by

MARK CRILLEY

A Dell Yearling Book

Published by
Dell Yearling
an imprint of
Random House Children's Books
a division of Random House, Inc.
New York

Visit us on the Web! www.randomhouse.com/kids

Educators and librarians, for a variety of teaching tools, visit us at www.randomhouse.com/teachers

ISBN: 0-440-41891-7

Reprinted by arrangement with Delacorte Press

Printed in the United States of America

June 2003

10 9 8 7 6 5 4 3 2 1

OPM

For my brothers,
Bob and Jeff

Read all of Akiko's adventures

ACKNOWLEDGMENTS

I want first and foremost to express deepest gratitude to my editor at Delacorte Press, Jennifer Wingertzahn, who gave me just the sort of advice I needed as I made my way through this strange little zoo of a story. Thanks also to Melissa Knight, Alison Kelly, Colleen Fellingham, and Barbara Perris. Thanks as always to Akiko's biggest fans at Sirius Entertainment: Robb Horan, Larry Salamone, and Mark Bellis. And, until next time, a big kiss and hug to my wife, Miki, and my son, Matthew.

Chapter 1

My name is Akiko. This is the story of my journey to the planet Quilk and all the crazy—and extremely dangerous—stuff that happened to me while I was there. I know, I know. A girl like me has no business going to other planets in the first place. I mean, I really ought to wait until I've at least finished elementary school. What can I say? I keep getting invited, and it's *very* hard to turn these people down.

It all started last fall, just a few weeks after the new school year began. I'd finally made it to the fifth grade. I liked most of my teachers. Homework was light. Things were going well. Then, one warm September afternoon when I least expected it, they came to get me. Sometimes I wonder what would have happened if I hadn't been at school that day. Maybe I'd have missed out on the whole adventure. Probably not, though. I think they would have found me one way or another.

Well, anyway . . .

That afternoon I was at school tidying things up after a meeting of the girls' safety patrol in a first-floor classroom at Middleton Elementary. As leader of the patrol, it was my duty to organize the meetings every month, which was actually a lot of fun, since our little get-togethers hardly ever had anything to do with safety. Mainly we just used them as an excuse to talk loudly and eat potato chips in a classroom without anyone yelling at us. Unfortunately this also meant that I was the only one left to throw stuff in the garbage and put all the chairs on top of the desks after the others had gone home. Leadership has its drawbacks.

I was just about finished when I noticed a big mop standing in the corner halfway across the room from the broom closet. It was one of those big old janitor's mops that looked as if the school had bought it back in

1919 or something. It had that horrible stink old mops have, the sort of smell that makes you really glad you're not a floor. I was going to just leave it there, but then someone might think I was the one who had forgotten to put it away, so I went over and dragged it across the room—it was pretty heavy because it was still soaking wet—and opened the broom-closet door with a good yank.

"Boo!"

I jumped back as quickly as I could, clutching the mop handle as if it were a weapon. A voice inside that closet had just booed me, and though I figured it was probably just that crazy Jimmy Hampton pulling a prank, I wasn't taking any chances.

"Scared ya," the strangely familiar voice said from somewhere back in the shadows, "didn' I?"

It was definitely not Jimmy Hampton.

Then I saw a head emerge from behind a stack of cardboard boxes. The spiky blue-black hair, the unshaven chin, the mischievous squinty eyes . . . Who could it be but Spuckler Boach?

"Spuckler!" I cried, shooting a glance out the window

to make sure no one could see him. "What in the world are you doing here?"

"Now, 'Kiko," Spuckler said as he stepped out into the classroom, "that ain't no way t' greet an old friend!"

He leaned over and gave me a great big bear hug that lifted me right up off the floor. I didn't have the faintest idea how he'd gotten there or why, but I sure was glad to see him. It had been several months since I'd returned from my first big adventure in outer space, and I couldn't count the number of times I'd dreamed about seeing my Smoovian friends again.

"Stand back an' lemme get a good look atcha!" Spuckler said, locking his fingers around my upper arms and thrusting me back a good yard or so. We looked each other up and down as if we hadn't met in years.

"Whoo doggy, girl, you're gettin' bigger! What are ya now, a college student or somethin'?"

"No, Spuckler," I laughed. "I've only just started fifth grade."

"Well now, close your eyes, Little Miss Fi'th Grader,"

4

he said, stepping back to the broom closet, " 'cause I got a big honkin' surprise for ya!"

"Uh-oh," I replied. "I don't like the sound of this. . . ."

"Close 'em, already!" he ordered.

I shut my eyes and waited. There was a muffled noise from somewhere inside the broom closet, followed by the faint sound of sneakers squeaking on the floor.

"All right, y' can open 'em now," Spuckler said finally.

I opened my eyes and saw . . . well, *me*.

It was the Akiko robot, the same one Bip and Bop had used before to replace me here on Earth while I was off having adventures on the planet Smoo. She was wearing the same clothes I was and looked exactly like me in every way. Okay, her *posture* was a little better than mine, but otherwise she was a perfect copy.

"Hi, uh . . . Akiko," I said to her.

"Hello, Akiko," she returned with a smile.

"Thanks again for taking my place last time," I said. "You did a really good job. Even my parents didn't know."

"You're very welcome," she replied. "It was my pleasure."

"Of course, there is the matter of that grade you got on my geography test," I added with a wink.

"I'm sorry, Akiko." The robot hung her head sheepishly. "This time I promise I'll get much better grades on all your tests."

"*This time?* Whoa! Wait a minute," I said, turning to Spuckler. "You're not here to take me to *Smoo* again, are you?"

"Naw, 'Kiko," Spuckler answered reassuringly. "You seen enough a Smoo t' last a lifetime."

I was relieved, but also just a tiny bit disappointed.

"That's good," I said, crossing the room and pulling the shades down over the windows. "I was afraid you had me lined up for another weird prince-rescuing mission or something."

"No missions, 'Kiko," Spuckler explained. "No work, neither. We're here t' take ya on vacation!"

"Vacation?"

"All expenses paid by King Froptoppit," Spuckler continued with a gleam in his eyes. "'S just his way of thankin' ya for all the trouble ya went through rescuin' his son."

"Gee, I don't know," I said. "My school doesn't go on vacation again until Christmas. . . ."

"What are ya, nuts?" Spuckler chuckled. "We got a look-alike 'Kiko here, li'l lady. You can take off school any time ya want."

I paced back and forth and stroked my chin while I thought it over. I have to admit, a little break from school sounded pretty good to me right then. There was that big history test coming up in Mrs. Riffin's class, for one thing.

"A vacation, eh?"

"Tha's right," Spuckler said, grinning. "A real humdinger, too: the planet Quilk! There ain't no place like it in the whole dang universe."

"Now *wait* a minute," I said, wagging an accusing finger in Spuckler's face. "You said you weren't here to take me to another planet this time."

"I said we wasn't goin' t' *Smoo*," Spuckler corrected. "I didn't say nothin' about the planet Quilk."

I squinted disapprovingly at him, then turned to the

robot Akiko, hoping she might back me up. She just smiled at me and blinked her Akiko-copy eyes.

"You could have at least sent me a letter or something first," I said to Spuckler, planting my hands on my hips. "Don't I even get a chance to pack?"

"Ya don't *need* t' pack, 'Kiko," Spuckler answered. "We got all the stuff ya need out in the ship."

"Ship?" I asked. "You came to Middleton Elementary in a spaceship?"

"Well, how the heck *else* were we supposed to get here? Hitchhikin'?"

"You people are crazy! What if somebody *saw* you?"

"Nobody saw us," Spuckler stated authoritatively. "Now c'mon, girl. We ain't got all day. "

I stood there in the middle of the classroom, arms folded, weighing my options for just a few more seconds.

School . . .

. . . vacation.

Earth . . .

. . . Quilk.

"Okay, okay," I said at last, grabbing my backpack off one of the desks and handing it to the robot Akiko.

"Now make sure you get a good grade on my history test next week, all right? If you get anything less than a B-plus we're going to have a little talk when I get back."

"Don't worry, Akiko," the robot replied with a strangely formal salute. "I'll do better this time. I've been studying."

I had a sudden vision of the Akiko robot back on Smoo, surrounded by copies of my textbooks, studying intently for all my classes. What a weird, *weird* life I've got.

I dug into my pocket and gave the Akiko robot my locker key.

"Don't lose this. It's a five-dollar fine to get it replaced."

The Akiko robot nodded solemnly and put the key in her pocket.

"All right, Spuckler, let's get out of here," I whispered, opening the classroom door and poking my head into the hallway to make sure no one would see us leave. "I'm taking some serious risks here. This had better be fun."

"It's *gonna* be fun," Spuckler declared triumphantly. "More fun than ya ever had in your whole life!"

Chapter 2

Spuckler and I left the robot Akiko in the classroom with instructions to wait there for ten more minutes and then go home and start posing as me. We snuck down the hallway to a short flight of stairs that led to the playground. Spuckler kept wanting to lead the way, but I insisted on going first to make sure the coast was clear. I think a janitor might have seen us, but he was too busy waxing the floor to notice anything unusual (If he'd seen Spuckler's peg leg, I'll bet *that* would have made him look twice).

I opened the door leading outside and took a quick peek around. The Middleton Elementary playground was practically empty except for two girls—sixth graders, I think—sitting on the monkey bars talking and laughing. They were both facing away from us, though, so I figured if we kept quiet, they wouldn't even know we were there. A whole bunch of kids were playing touch football way over on the other side of the school, but they were too far away to pay us any mind. So we stepped outside and walked along the playground fence until we came to a spot near the back of the school where they put all the garbage. We climbed the fence and snuck back to a place where no one could see us, not even the girls on the monkey bars. There in the shadows, tucked between one of the Dumpsters and a windowless brick wall, was a bright, shiny blue-and-red spaceship!

It was just like the one that had taken me to Smoo several months before, with the same flame-emblazoned tail fins and—strange but true—no roof whatsoever. In the front seat was Spuckler's robot, Gax, who squeaked and buzzed happily as soon as he saw me.

"HELLO, AKIKO," said Gax. "HOW WONDERFUL IT IS TO SEE YOU AGAIN."

"Thanks, Gax," I replied. "Did you get an oil change or something? You look good."

He made several happy popping noises and rocked gently from side to side.

Just above Gax was Poog, as round and purple as ever, hovering in midair like a helium balloon.

"Hi, Poog!" I said, seeing a reflection of myself in each of his big glassy eyes. "How're you doing?"

He smiled, floated down a little closer to my face, and said something in that gurgly, warbly language of his. I have no idea what it meant, but I could tell by looking at him that he was doing just fine. He looked almost as pleased to see me as I was to see him.

In the backseat was Mr. Beeba. He was so nervous about being on the planet Earth, he looked as if he was going to faint in relief at my arrival.

"Climb aboard, Akiko!" he whispered excitedly, motioning wildly with his oversized hands. "Time is of the essence! We were spotted a moment ago by a pair of small brown-haired quadrupeds! No doubt they'll be returning soon, armed to the teeth and in greater numbers. . . ."

"Those were probably just a couple of stray dogs, Mr. Beeba," I said, trying my best to reassure him. "I don't think we have to worry about them carrying weapons."

"Are you sure?" Mr. Beeba asked doubtfully, still staring at a spot where he evidently expected the animals to reappear at any moment. "They looked none too pleased to see us. I had the distinct impression that we had somehow violated one of their most sacred cultural taboos."

I chuckled and turned back to the others.

"Boy, it sure is great seeing you guys again," I said. "Did you have any trouble finding Middleton Elementary?"

"Well t' tell th' truth, we did stop at a different school first by mistake," Spuckler said with a wink. "Almost grabbed a little blond-haired girl 'stead of you just t' save time. . . ."

"Ha ha ha," I said, rolling my eyes and climbing into the backseat next to Mr. Beeba.

"They're back!" Mr. Beeba shrieked in a panic, pointing frantically at two very confused-looking cats staring from the top of one of the Dumpsters. "Quickly, Spuckler, *quickly!"*

"Will ya calm down, ya little goofball?" Spuckler said, revving the ship's engine. "Now hang on tight, 'Kiko," he added as he pushed a few buttons on the dashboard, "'cause we're gonna be hightailin' it outta here pretty darn quick."

He wasn't kidding: That spaceship took off like a bottle rocket! We shot up over the roof in no time at all, sending dozens of pigeons whirling in all directions.

I had just a second or two to catch a dizzying view of Middleton before we were suddenly way up above the clouds, racing higher and higher into the bright blue sky. I was still a little confused about the fact that there was air in outer space—I couldn't help wishing they'd brought along a helmet just in case—but just as before, there was plenty of air no matter how high we went. The blue sky turned purple and then black as we zoomed out into the stars, Earth shrinking behind us at an alarming rate.

"Jeez, guys," I said as I watched my planet disappear into the blackness, "what's the big rush?"

"The planet Quilk is very far away, Akiko," Mr. Beeba explained, handing me a shiny brochure. "It could take us a whole *day* to get there if we don't speed things up a bit."

I opened the brochure and examined the brightly colored images inside. There were pictures of all sorts of strange-looking alien animals of all shapes and sizes, surrounded by blocks of text in some weird language that looked like it was written diagonally rather than left to right.

"Sorry there are no English translations," Mr. Beeba said apologetically. "They evidently don't get many visitors from Earth."

"So what's the big deal about Quilk?" I asked. "Is it more interesting than Smoo?"

"Strictly speaking, no," Mr. Beeba answered in his best teacherly voice. "But it is home to one of the most extensive zoological parks in the entire universe, and as such it presents a marvelous opportunity for intensive study and personal edification on a truly grand scale."

"Edjufication?" Spuckler responded with an indignant snort. "Beebs, we're goin' on a *holiday* here. Why don't ya give the big words a rest and jus' enjoy yourself a little?"

"For your information, Spuckler," Mr. Beeba replied, "these so-called big words are in and of themselves a source of *profound* enjoyment for those of us who possess the mental faculties to make proper use of them."

"Yeah, well, you're givin' *my* mental faculties a major headache," said Spuckler, "so put a *cork* in it for a while, will ya?"

"You guys," I said, folding my hands behind my head and leaning back into the soft red cushions of the backseat, "you haven't changed a bit."

"You sound as if you wish we *had*, Akiko," Mr. Beeba replied with a sniff.

"Oh no, Mr. B.," I said, smiling and taking in the view as we whizzed farther and farther from Earth. "I like you all just the way you are."

Chapter 3

We flew through space at an incredible speed, past huge glowing galaxies and over fields of enormous spinning asteroids. Spuckler and Mr. Beeba argued about all kinds of things, asking for my opinion every once in a while but hardly ever waiting to actually hear it. Gax sat contentedly in the front seat, slowly pivoting his head this way and that, scanning the universe for who knows what. Poog floated near my shoulder humming a quiet little tune, a strange melody that kept repeating over and over but somehow never sounded quite the same.

I stared at the brochure Mr. Beeba had given me, wondering about the zoo we'd be visiting on the planet Quilk. What would it be like? I hadn't been to very many zoos on Earth, much less one on another planet, so I really didn't know what to expect. One thing was sure: It would be a whole lot more interesting than staying at home and studying for my history test. I folded up the brochure and stuck it in my pocket, then closed my eyes and tried to get a little rest.

After what seemed like three or four hours, Spuckler began to slow the ship down a little.

"We should be comin' up on Quilk any minute now," he announced. "Better take it slow or we might scoot right on past it an' never know the differ'nce."

Within seconds the planet Quilk came into view. It was a little ball of a planet, surrounded by swatches of soft yellow-orange clouds. As we came closer, though, I began to see that it wasn't quite as round as it had first appeared. One side was perfectly flat, as if a third of the planet had been sliced off with an enormous knife.

"Quilk is a remarkable feat of engineering, Akiko," Mr. Beeba explained. "Mr. Yunk, the owner of the

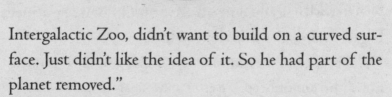

Intergalactic Zoo, didn't want to build on a curved surface. Just didn't like the idea of it. So he had part of the planet removed."

"*Removed?* No way!" I said, taking everything in with wide eyes. Our ship dove into the clouds and reemerged underneath them.

"Don't ask me how they did it," Mr. Beeba said with a shudder. "The lengths some people will go to in the name of commerce . . . It's quite beyond me, I assure you."

As Spuckler guided the spaceship down for a landing, we were treated to a spectacular view of the zoo. It was gigantic! It filled almost the entire flattened side of the planet, with all the remaining space being taken up by silvery skyscraper hotels and parking lots packed with all kinds of spacefaring vehicles. Just before the ship touched down, I was able to see over the walls of the park and catch a brief glimpse of the multicolored world held within them. There were tall blue-and-orange towers and rows and rows of swaying purple palm trees. There were vast circular plazas connected by wide golden boulevards, all of which were teeming with visitors rushing excitedly from one exhibit to the next. Some people viewed the zoo from the luxury of gigantic floating tour buses, while others rode on the backs of many-legged camel-like animals that wove gracefully through the crowds like swans on the surface of a pond. I was dying to get inside and have a look around!

Spuckler brought our ship to a stop at the best parking spot we could find, which was almost half a mile away from the entrance.

"Wow! This is one popular place," I said, climbing out of the ship and staring with dread at the seemingly endless line of people waiting to get in.

Gax made a squeaky whining sound and Poog's mouth turned decidedly downward at the edges. Even robots and aliens don't much care for waiting in lines, I guess.

"Well, there's no use standin' around gripin'," Spuckler said, marching off to join a group of aliens with arms like octopuses at the end of the line. "Let's get on over there and pay our dues like ever'body else."

"Thankfully I had the foresight to bring along some reading material," Mr. Beeba said smugly, drawing a leather-bound book from beneath his belt and waving it under my nose. "Shtunk & Hortleton's *Guide to Interplanetary Irrigation Theory*. Gripping stuff. I'll read it aloud if you like."

"Uh, no thanks, Mr. Beeba," I answered as we joined Spuckler at the end of the line, still at least a quarter of a mile from the entrance.

"Suit yourself," Mr. Beeba replied, adjusting his spectacles a bit before burying his nose in the thick little book.

We stood there in the parking lot for about half an hour. The line was hardly moving at all. Once, everyone actually moved four or five steps *backward*, causing a collective groan to rise from the line. Spuckler began voicing complaints to no one in particular, claiming that the zoo was not all it was cracked up to be and naming other places where we'd be better off spending our time. Gax kept stretching his neck to its maximum length, raising his head above the crowd to see what was holding things up. He was never able to come up with any good explanation, though. Poog hummed quietly to himself, this time choosing a sluggish melody that seemed to go back and start all over again every few seconds. Only Mr. Beeba remained oblivious to it all, lost in the evidently fascinating world of interplanetary irrigation.

I was about to sit down on the ground just to give my legs a rest when suddenly I noticed a little monkey-like creature working his way from the front of the line to the back. He was about three feet tall, with blue-gray fur and a head that looked a little too small for his body. He had big black eyes and a little monkey nose, but his yellow lips protruded from his face and came to a point almost like a beak. He wore an orange-and-green cap on his head, with a matching vest that fit snugly around his upper body. He had reddish three-toed claws for feet and a long furry tail that curled around this way and that as he moved from one visitor to the next. He was clutching a photo in one paw, consulting it every so often as he studied the faces of those in line.

Poog had noticed him too, and he turned to me and smiled as the creature drew nearer. It was a weird smile—a slightly worried smile somehow—and I began to wonder what Poog was trying to tell me. I knew better than to ask. Poog always seemed to prefer letting me figure things out for myself.

When the creature came to our place in the line, he stopped right in front of me and scrutinized my face with great care. He raised the photo with an outstretched paw and squinted one eye, throwing the other wide open so that he could compare my face to the one in the photo. His little round eye darted back and forth several times; then he straightened himself up, removed his cap with a swift movement of one paw, and bowed gracefully before me like a servant to a queen.

"*Udplut bluk-bluk! Ibdibble chut-chubble!*" he said in a high-pitched squeak of a voice. "*Hib-dib, hib-dib, hib-dib.*"

He replaced the cap on his head, stepped back, and extended one arm in the direction of the park. He froze in that position, eyes to the ground, patiently waiting.

"Did you catch any of that, Mr. Beeba?" I asked.

"*Ahem.* Yes, well, er . . . ," he replied, closing the little book and tucking it under his belt, ". . . this is not a dialect of the Quilkan tongue with which I am terribly familiar, I'm afraid. I can tell you that his placement of gerunds is highly unorthodox, and I do have a bone to pick with all of his dangling participles. . . ."

"Yeah, but what the heck is he *sayin'*, Beebs?" Spuckler asked impatiently.

"I haven't the faintest idea," Mr. Beeba admitted.

"Well, where I come from," I said, "this would look an awful lot like someone trying to escort us to the front of the line."

"An interesting interpretation," Mr. Beeba replied. "However—"

"I like your way of thinkin', 'Kiko," Spuckler cheerfully interrupted, slapping me on the back and stepping out to a spot in the parking lot just behind the monkey creature. "Now come on, girl. Let's get movin' b'fore he changes his mind!"

I turned to Poog. He smiled, nodded, and floated over to join Spuckler and the monkey creature. Gax followed suit, leaving Mr. Beeba and me the only ones still in line.

"Okay," I said, stepping forward and moving cautiously into a position at the head of the newly formed group, "but don't blame me if we get seriously yelled at for cutting."

"Hib-dib, hib-dib," said the monkey creature, and off we all went.

Chapter 4

The monkey creature ceremoniously led us straight past the hundreds of jealous people in line to a lively crowd gathered at the main entrance. It was a whirl of motion and noise: potbellied aliens hawking plastic T-shirts, shady-looking characters scalping tickets, and harried zoo employees at the entrance booths making change in what looked like dozens of different currencies.

I braced myself to plunge right into the mayhem, but the monkey creature led us away from the main entrance to a large door about a hundred feet to the left. He gave the door several quick taps with a curled-up paw. A little window in the door opened, and two greenish eyes peered out.

"*Blib frub nub-nubbit!*" the monkey creature cried angrily, gesturing impatiently in my direction.

The green eyes focused on me for a moment, then disappeared into the darkness behind the door. A moment later there was a series of loud clicks, followed by one very loud bang. The door flew open and the monkey creature stepped confidently inside, motioning politely to us that we were to go with him.

I went in first, followed by Spuckler, Poog, Gax, and Mr. Beeba. Our monkey-creature escort led us past a tall furry figure on our left: the doorkeeper with the green eyes. He wore a cap and vest identical to the monkey creature's except that his were many sizes larger (and they *still* looked a little small on him). He'd have been really scary if not for the fact that he was bowing to me like crazy and smiling with all his might.

The monkey creature said a few more words to us in his mumbly language as he led us down a dimly lit corridor and up a long flight of polished marble steps. It was like a spiral staircase that couldn't make up its mind, curving first to the left, then to the right, then coming to a stop before a gigantic wooden door at least two or three stories above the one we'd come from. This door was apparently left unlocked, because the monkey creature simply gave it a good push and it slowly swung open without making the slightest noise.

"Pibblig pig f'nibnig!" the monkey creature said with a bow, smartly tipping his cap before leaping through the doorway and dashing across the carpeted floor of the room in front of us.

It was a large rectangular space, brightly lit by sunlight pouring through a wall of windows on the far end. The whole room was decked out in green and gold, with polished golden statues lining the walls and a humongous emerald-studded chandelier hanging from the ceiling. Giant chairs and sofas were carefully arranged in neat semicircles, each surrounded by golden-potted plants and tables topped with shaded lamps and big bowls of fruit. It all stood on a plush carpet of pool-table green that seemed to silence our footsteps before we even made them.

Silhouetted against the windows was a man seated at an enormous wooden desk. The monkey creature sped noiselessly across the carpet, leaped over the desk, and landed gracefully on the hulking figure's shoulder. The man then stood up, creating an impressive black shape against the wall of sunlight behind him. He was about twice the size of an average adult. The glare prevented me from making out his facial features, but a glint of wire at the edge of his face suggested that he was wearing glasses.

"Come in, my friends, come in!" the man said, his voice slightly nasal and pleasantly raspy. "Welcome to the Intergalactic Zoo!"

We all took a few hesitant steps onto the carpet, inching our way into the room. The man stepped out from behind the desk and crossed the room in a few confident strides. As he moved away from the blinding sunlight, his features became easier to see.

He was a heavyset man—even a little fat, I'd have to say—dressed from head to toe in silky, expensive-

looking clothes. He wore a neatly trimmed mustache
and beard and round wire-rimmed glasses that rested
high on a reddish, pockmarked nose. His hair was thin-
ning almost to the point of being completely gone, but
his double chin and expressive eyes created the effect of
a little boy's face. He looked as if he were coming out
to play.

"Allow me to introduce myself," he said as he came to a stop before us. He was fully twice as tall as Spuckler, maybe even bigger. "I am Norvis Yunk, founder and proprietor of the Quilkan Intergalactic Zoo. I see you have already met Wolo."

Wolo, still perched on Yunk's shoulder, grinned and made a little chirping noise from his position high above us.

"P-pleased to meet you, Mr. Yunk," I said, trying not to stare at him as I spoke. "My name is Akiko. This is Spuckler Boach, Mr. Beeba, Gax, and Poog."

"What a pleasure it is to meet you all," he replied, bending his knees so that he could greet each of us face to face. "Do call me Norvis, won't you?"

He looked as if he was a very kindhearted man who went to great lengths to prevent his sheer size from frightening people.

"Have a seat, now," he said, leading us over to a bunch of chairs on one side of the room. "You've had quite a long journey. You must be exhausted."

We all sat down as best we could. The furniture was

much too big for us, and our legs dangled high above the floor.

"King Froptoppit asked me to give you all the royal treatment," Yunk explained, "so I sent Wolo out to make sure you didn't end up standing in line like everyone else." He said the words *everyone else* as if he were talking about a herd of cattle. Clearly he thought we were something special.

"Are you a friend of King Froptoppit?" I asked.

"Well, not exactly," Yunk answered. "He did contribute some marvelous Smoovian Groot Owls to my collection some years ago, though, and for that I am eternally grateful."

He turned to Mr. Beeba with a look of recognition forming in his eyes.

"Why, if I'm not mistaken, *you* had a hand in that transaction, Mr. Beeba. . . ."

Mr. Beeba smiled nostalgically.

"Yes, well, I wasn't going to say anything," he replied in an exaggerated show of modesty, "but now that *you* have—"

"So when's the tour begin, Norvis?" Spuckler interrupted. "We ain't got all day, y' know."

"Spuckler!" I whispered angrily.

"You're quite right, Mr. Boach," Yunk replied with a chuckle. "It does us no good to sit here yakking all day." He rose from his chair and grabbed a walking stick from a case against the wall.

"Let's get out there and see the animals!"

Chapter 5

Norvis Yunk led us out of the room by way of a door near his desk, tapping lightly on the steps with his walking stick as we made our way down another flight of stairs. Wolo was still on his shoulder, and every once in a while Yunk would dig into one of his oversized pockets and produce a biscuit for Wolo to chew on. They reminded me a little of my grandma Mina and her fluffy cat, Tama. Well, apart from the fact that Yunk and Wolo were three or four times bigger, of course.

We came to a place at the bottom of the stairs where only a pair of wide brass gates stood between us and the rest of the park. As we approached, Wolo leaped off Yunk's shoulder, grabbed a ring of keys from the wall, and swiftly unlocked the gates. He took his place back on his master's shoulder as Yunk threw the gates open and ushered us into the Intergalactic Zoo.

"From Uz-Paloo to Vorga-2," Yunk said cheerfully, evidently quoting from a favorite poem, *"there's naught compares with a day at the zoo!"*

It's hard to describe the feeling I had during those first few moments inside. I guess you just have to imagine a zoo without cages, without walls, without even boundary lines between the visitors and the animals being viewed. Towering long-necked blue creatures roamed freely through the crowds, while multilegged furry ones snaked this way and that. Flocks of multicolored reptile-birds soared high above our heads, occasionally swooping down and landing on the backs of enormous pink hippo-beasts that moved so slowly they hardly seemed to be moving at all. And everywhere were the happy tourists who had come from far and wide to see the zoo, some of them so strange-looking they seemed more like residents than visitors. There were at least five kinds of music playing simultaneously, and several different food smells—some good, some bad, some just plain *stinky*—that filled my nostrils and made me feel hungry and queasy at the same time. It was a little overwhelming, if you want to know the truth.

Yunk whispered something to Wolo that caused him to chirp happily and dash off into the crowds.

"Our transportation," Yunk explained. "The park's become so crowded recently, I'm afraid trying to see it all on foot is now a rather foolhardy proposition, to say nothing of the blisters you'd get." There was a gleam in his eyes when he described these problems, as if they were in fact the very things he'd worked all his life to achieve.

"Quite, quite," Mr. Beeba agreed, no doubt approving of Yunk's vocabulary as much as anything else.

A minute or two later Wolo returned. Or rather, a forty-foot-tall orange lizard-elephant-thing returned in his place. It lumbered through the crowds on its surprisingly small feet, each movement followed by the gentle jingling of tiny bells on its tasseled saddle. The beast's head was wide and low to the ground, with four shiny black eyes that rolled slowly back and forth under half-closed lids. Its mouth was flanked by two curved yellow tusks that jutted three or four feet in front of it, gently nudging passersby aside as it made its way toward us. Great puffs of purplish smoke blew out of its nostrils every time it exhaled, accompanied by a strange wheezing noise that sounded more or less like a broken accordion. It was only after craning my neck and squinting up at the fancy compartment on its back that I realized Wolo was *riding* the thing, steering it with a complicated system of ropes and pulleys.

Poog smiled approvingly, while Mr. Beeba blinked in awe. Gax quivered a bit and scooted quickly backward on his rusty wheels, looking as if he feared he might accidentally get stepped on.

"*Yeeeeeee*-hawdy!" Spuckler cried. "A Jullba lizard! A real live *Jullba* lizard!"

"A *spotted* Jullba lizard," Yunk corrected him. "One of only twenty-seven in the universe," he added proudly, "twenty-three of which reside within the confines of this zoo."

"Man-oh-man-oh-man!" Spuckler continued, working himself up into a frenzy. "I ain't seen one of these since my ranchin' days on the moons of Jagoozi."

"I've had my *eyes* on those

41

Jagoozi ones for some time now," Yunk responded grumpily, "but the owners refuse to sell."

"Well, what're we waitin' for?" said Spuckler as he lifted a very nervous-looking Gax with both hands, tucked him awkwardly under one arm, and strode confidently back to the Jullba lizard's long orange tail. "Let's get goin'!"

"Spuckler!" Mr. Beeba scolded. "You can't go gallivanting about as if you *own* the place. . . ."

"But of *course* he can," Yunk said with a grin. "It's the only way to see this zoo, as far as I'm concerned."

By that time Spuckler and Gax had made their way up the Jullba lizard's back and were halfway inside the passengers' compartment. Poog simply floated directly up to his preferred spot right behind Wolo's shoulder. Yunk invited Mr. Beeba and me to climb up the tail just as Spuckler had. Needless to say, it was a whole lot harder than Spuckler made it look.

"Man, it's hard to get a *grip* on this thing," I said as one of my sneakered feet shot off to one side, leaving me hugging the tail desperately with both arms. "It's a good thing Yunk put a riding thingie up there or else we'd be in serious trouble."

"Howdah," Mr. Beeba said from behind me with a muffled grunt (he clearly wasn't having any easier a time than I was). "It's called a howdah. Not a 'riding thingie.'"

Finally, with a bit of help from Yunk, we all made it into our seats. Yunk himself sat right in front next to Wolo and gave orders on where we were to go first. Wolo translated Yunk's commands into a few loud whistles and several tugs on one of the ropes. A moment later the Jullba lizard slowly moved forward through the crowds below, and so began our grand tour of the Intergalactic Zoo.

Chapter 6

I wish I could tell you about every single one of the animals we saw that day, but I honestly can't. There were so many you'd be begging me to stop before I even got through a fraction of them. There were great big balloon-like animals that inflated and deflated every few seconds, stretching out as tight as drums and then quickly shriveling up like prunes. There were liquidy creatures that wiggled and slid through the air as if they had hardly any weight at all (which was probably the case, since you could see right through them). There were one-legged beasts that bounced up and down like pogo sticks and others—furry and orange—that rolled from place to place like windblown beach balls. There were animals with twenty heads and animals with no heads at all. Some were so small we had to climb off the Jullba lizard and get down on our hands and knees just to see them. Others were so big *they* had to get down on their hands and knees just to see *us.* There was simply every kind of animal you can imagine, and there were hundreds of others you'd never imagine in a thousand years. And Yunk assured us that we still hadn't seen them all.

After a few hours Yunk ordered the Jullba lizard to stop, announcing that it was time for lunch.

"All *riiight,*" Spuckler cheered. "Lookin' at all these weird critters has worked up my appetite somethin' fierce."

Yunk gave Wolo a few detailed instructions, sending him scampering off for food. While he was gone, Yunk continued to introduce us to all the animals as they passed by.

"See that one?" Yunk asked me, pointing to a pancake-shaped creature that whirled through the air like a slow-motion Frisbee. "A spinning Whim-blitzer. You can't see one of those on Smoo, can you?"

"No way," I answered, wondering if the things kept spinning even when they slept. "I'm not really sure about that, though," I added. "I'm not *from* Smoo, you know."

"You're not?" Yunk asked.

"No, I'm from the planet Earth," I explained.

"Earth?" Yunk asked, his eyes opening wide in astonishment. "You mean you're . . . ," he continued, focusing his eyes intently on me, ". . . an Earthian?"

"I think the proper term is Earth*ling*," I answered.

"Goodness gracious," he said, removing his glasses to examine me up close. "You *are* an Earthian, aren't you?" (Who knows? Maybe Earthling *isn't* the proper term after all.)

"Yeah," I replied, wishing he wouldn't stick his big face quite so close to mine. "We're not that rare, you know. There are lots of, uh, Earth-i-ans . . . just like me . . . ," I added, scooting back as far as I could. "You know, on *Earth*."

"Akiko's not just *any* Earthian," Mr. Beeba said proudly, eager to join the conversation. "She's the brightest, cleverest, bravest Earthian there is!"

"Oh, go on," I said, blushing. "I'm just a regular kid, really."

"Who'd have thought," Yunk whispered, a faraway look in his eyes. "An Earthian, right under my nose."

"But Mr. Yunk, surely you've seen Earthians before," said Mr. Beeba. "I'd have thought a man of your expertise would have visited Earth many times by now."

"Hm?" Yunk replied, clearly lost in thought.

"I said, I'd have thought a man of your expertise—"

"Oh yes!" Yunk said abruptly, shaking his head as if to bring himself back from a dream. "Yes, quite. Earthians are very common in my business, exceedingly common," he added, turning back to me apologetically, "if you'll pardon the expression."

Just then Wolo returned, followed by a crew of five little blue-haired creatures carrying silver platters loaded with food. They arranged the platters in the center of the compartment, bowed politely, and marched down the Jullba's tail in an orderly procession.

"Eat! Eat!" Yunk said with a wave of his hands. "This zoo cannot be properly enjoyed on an empty stomach!"

He didn't need to repeat himself. Spuckler, Mr. Beeba, and I dug in with both hands, feeding ourselves and smacking our lips like a pack of hungry wolves. There were thick multicolored sandwiches and black crispy things that crunched like potato chips but tasted like meat. There were bright red vegetables with edible purple seeds and a wonderful salad made of sphere-shaped leaves that popped like balloons when you bit into them. There were large fleshy fruits as juicy and sweet as mangos and little blue eggs filled with something that tasted an awful lot like chocolate.

Gax and Poog looked on with fascination, as if the very idea of eating was quite foreign to them, and the ferocity with which we ate made it seem all the more amusing. As for Yunk, he took just a few select morsels from each plate, savoring them like little delicacies. In this way he was able to continue enjoying the meal long after the rest of us had fallen back in a stuffed-belly stupor.

Yunk passed around little glasses of sweet green-colored tea at the end of the meal. This was no doubt intended to revive us. Without it we'd all surely have curled up for a long afternoon nap. Then the little blue-haired creatures reappeared, speedily clearing away the platters and what little traces of food remained on them.

"Now for the most amazing animal of all," Yunk said dramatically as Wolo started the Jullba lizard moving again, "my newest acquisition: the glowing Fillaprims of the planet Myoont!"

Chapter 7

"**Fillaprims!**" Mr. Beeba gasped. "Here? In this park?"

"Yes," Yunk replied with a grin. "A bit of a coup on my part, I must say."

"We're in for a treat, Akiko," said Mr. Beeba gleefully. "Fillaprims are among the rarest animals in the universe. And *glowing* Fillaprims . . . why, they're the stuff of legends. Hardly anyone has ever seen them up close. Myoont is such a dreadfully hard place to get to, for one thing."

The Jullba lizard carried us through the crowds to a large iron gate flanked by two ornate booths. As we approached, two beefy guards stepped out of the booths and dutifully opened the gates.

"This area is off limits to all but the most special guests," Yunk said to me in a half-whisper as the Jullba lizard carried us past the saluting guards. "It's where I keep animals that are not yet ready for public view."

We continued for many minutes, riding through this strangely quiet and empty section of the park. It was much more like a wealthy private estate than a zoo. Vast green lawns stretched out on either side of us, and carefully manicured trees lined the roads. There was no sign of animals anywhere. Some distance before us stood a many-storied tower, tall and cylindrical like a giant chess piece, capped by a vast mansion of white stone walls and gently sloping orange rooftops. It was like a palace lifted out of a fairy tale and set on its own stately pedestal.

"That's where *I* live," Yunk said with a wink, clearly very proud of the unique residence he'd created for himself. "I'm keeping the Fillaprims down in the basement. They're very sensitive creatures, you see, known to literally vanish into thin air at the sight of intruders."

"So how'n the heck're we gonna get a peek at 'em?" asked Spuckler.

"I've devised a small chamber from which one can view them remotely through a deftly arranged labyrinth of mirrors," Yunk explained mysteriously. "Even then they are capable of detecting the presence of large groups of strangers, so I'm afraid I'll have to take you in one at a time."

"A wise precaution," Mr. Beeba said, nodding knowingly.

Soon we arrived at the foot of the tower, and Norvis Yunk invited us all to step down from the Jullba lizard.

Unfortunately, going back down the Jullba's tail was no easier than climbing up it. Miraculously, Mr. Beeba and I made it to the ground without breaking our necks.

Yunk led us all to a small pair of doors that opened diagonally into the base of the tower, like one of those tornado shelters you see in the movies. It seemed more like the entrance to a dungeon than the gateway to a magical animal exhibit. Yunk produced a key from his pocket and undid the heavy lock that held the doors shut.

"Ubnug fib-lib," he said to Wolo in hushed tones. *"Norglig lig-lig org-lig."*

Wolo looked at me, then looked back at his master. He had a startled and confused expression on his face.

"Org-lig?" he asked.

"Org . . . lig . . . ," Yunk repeated, pronouncing each word with great care.

Wolo raised his eyebrows, then nodded slowly. He opened the doors, slipped inside, and closed them carefully behind him.

"Wolo's going to make sure the Fillaprims are ready to be viewed," Yunk explained with a smile.

There was a long pause as we waited for Wolo to return. I couldn't help thinking that Yunk seemed nervous about something. Was he worried about the Fillaprims? Maybe he thought they'd disappear before we got a chance to see them. I don't know, though. It was as if he was thinking about something else altogether.

"Thank you, Mr. Yunk," I said, reaching up to touch his sleeve.

"Mm?" was all he could manage to say. "Why . . . whatever for, my dear child?"

"Oh, I don't know, just for all the incredible things you've shown us today," I answered. "I mean, I'm sure you've got lots of better things to do than play tour guide for me and my friends."

"Not at all, Akiko," he replied with a slightly unnatural smile. "Spending the day with you is an opportunity I wouldn't trade for anything."

Suddenly the doors opened a crack and out popped Wolo, who jumped up and stuffed something into Yunk's pocket. I didn't get a chance to see what it was, but for a moment I caught a whiff of a very strange smell, almost like something from a chemistry set.

"Excellent!" Yunk said, clapping his hands together. "Now we can go in."

"All right!" Spuckler said, stepping forward eagerly.

"Hold on there, my good man," Yunk said, reaching out to restrain Spuckler. "I've got to take you in one at a time, remember? Since Akiko is the guest of honor, I believe it's only proper that I take her in first."

"Aww," moaned Spuckler, sounding like a disappointed schoolboy.

"You're quite right, Mr. Yunk," said Beeba, grabbing Spuckler by the elbow and pulling him aside. "Ladies first, as they say, heh heh . . ."

"Come along, Akiko," Yunk said, lifting Wolo up to his shoulder with one hand and taking me by the arm with the other. "You're really going to love this."

I turned my head and caught one last glimpse of Spuckler, Mr. Beeba, Gax, and Poog before we left them behind and descended the stairway into the darkness.

"We'll be right back!" I called to them before they vanished from view.

"Take as long as you like," I heard Mr. Beeba call cheerfully. "This is an experience you'll never forget!"

Norvis Yunk, Wolo, and I made our way down the steps to a dark, humid passageway somewhere underneath the tower. The farther we went, the darker it got.

"Mr. Yunk," I said, "aren't there any, uh, lights down here?"

"Oh yes, Akiko," came his reply, "but we mustn't switch them on, you see. It'll frighten the Fillaprims." His voice was now very tense, almost shaky. Suddenly I realized I had no interest at all in seeing these weird

58

animals. I really wanted to turn around and go back. I considered asking if we could just forget about the whole thing, but . . . I don't know, I guess I just didn't want to cause trouble.

We continued farther and farther down the corridor, which was now so dark I could hardly see anything at all. Before long I had nothing to go on but my own sense of balance and Yunk's giant hand pulling me along into the blackness.

"Here we are," whispered Yunk as he came to a stop. I heard the jangling of keys and a scraping metallic noise that I imagined was a door being unlocked. I hoped this would result in better lighting, but the corridor seemed if anything even darker than before.

"Is this where I get to see the Fillaprims?" I asked.

There was no response. Yunk's hand closed more tightly around my own.

"Mr. Yunk?"

Silence.

"Mr. Yu—"

Suddenly I felt Yunk's hand clap firmly over my mouth while his other arm swept around my body. I tried to scream but was unable to make any noise louder than a muffled squeak. A second later I felt a damp piece of cloth over my nose and mouth and my nostrils were filled with a horrible chemical smell—like ammonia, only worse. I began to feel dizzy almost immediately.

"*Oblug,*" I heard Yunk whisper to Wolo as my head began to spin. "*Nib-lig nib-lig . . .*"

A moment later I was out cold.

Chapter 8

When I awoke, I saw nothing but a bright light shining down on me. I was feeling very groggy, and it was a while before I even had the strength to keep my eyes open for more than a few seconds at a time. I sat up and rubbed my face furiously, trying to force myself to wake up. Judging by how hungry I was, a great many hours had passed since I'd fallen unconscious.

Little by little the details of my surroundings became clearer to me. I was on top of a large round table about ten feet in diameter. But I wasn't *directly* on the table. I was actually seated on a polished disc of

cherry-red wood. Everywhere I turned, I saw a faint reflection of myself: I was surrounded on all sides by a tall dome of perfectly clear glass. There was just enough space for me to stand up, which I did, but only briefly, since it made me feel dizzy. The air was a little stuffy yet still breathable, thanks to a circle of small holes at the top of the dome.

"Spuckler?" I called out. "Mr. Beeba?"

There was no answer. Somehow I knew that they were nowhere nearby, that I was really and truly on my own this time. I had a sudden panicky feeling just then, a feeling—no, a *certainty*—that I was in the worst sort of trouble. My heart started pounding like mad, and my stomach was turning flips inside me. I curled myself up into a ball and just sat there shaking uncontrollably for a minute or two. I wasn't crying yet, but I was pretty close.

I shut my eyes and tried to imagine Spuckler and Gax and Mr. Beeba and Poog being there with me. I tried to think of what they might say.

"C-calm down, 'Kiko," I said to myself, doing my best imitation of Spuckler. "This ain't no time to f-freak out on us." Somehow just imagining what he would say seemed to relax me a little.

"Yes, Akiko, do keep things in perspective," I continued, trying to imitate the teacherly voice of Mr. Beeba. "It does us no good to have you"—how would he put it?—"taking leave of your senses like this."

I was going to try to impersonate Gax and Poog, too,

but I didn't want to push my luck. Besides, I was already past the worst of the panic, and my heartbeat was slowing down to something closer to normal.

I looked through the glass, beyond the tabletop, and examined the rest of the room. It was a large, dimly lit space with dark wooden paneling along the lower half of the walls and red floral-patterned paper covering the upper half. One wall was given over to the heads of various alien beasts mounted on wooden plaques, like antlered animals in a hunter's trophy room. On another wall was a crackling fire in a fireplace surrounded by a great stone hearth. A third wall was almost entirely taken up by velvety green curtains. In the middle of the ceiling was a large skylight through which I could see a starry, moonless sky.

All around were tables just like mine—at least a dozen of them, I'd say—each with a glass dome on top, lit from above by individual beams of yellow light. Beneath every dome stood a different alien being, each with two arms and two legs, some dressed in elaborate costumes and standing proudly with heads held high, others posed with weapons in hand as if in the midst of battle. They were all lifeless, like stuffed animals, which somehow made them all the more frightening. I felt as if I was in the middle of a really creepy alien museum.

Which I *was,* really. I mean, every table had a little placard on it describing what sort of alien was inside the dome and what planet it had come from and giving the Latin name for its species. Whoever had set this place up was very well organized.

Suddenly the panicky feeling came back, much stronger this time: It caught me totally by surprise. Within seconds there were tears streaming down my face. I jumped to my feet and threw myself up against the glass, making crazy smears and streaks with my fingers.

"Heeeeellllp!" I screamed at the top of my lungs, pounding now with clenched red fists. "You . . . you've gotta help me! You've gotta let me out of here!"

There was only silence.

No doubt about it. I was completely alone.

"M-Mr. Yunk!" I screamed. I was really blubbering now, just like a little baby. "Somebody . . . *anybody . . .*"

"Oh, for crying out loud," I heard a voice say. "Will

you take it *easy*?" It was a high-pitched voice, feminine-sounding, and it came from somewhere very nearby.

I spun around, wiping the tears from my eyes as quickly as I could. There, on another round table just a few feet away from mine, was . . . a girl. But not a girl, exactly. She was an alien. A *girl* alien.

She was very pretty, with a small, pale green face, round brown eyes, and little orange lips. Her long shiny hair, which gradually changed from black at the roots to violet at the tips, flowed all the way down to the backs of her legs. Her slim body was cloaked in an elegant dress of gold and purple, and her long neck was encircled by a silver necklace from which hung a beautifully polished piece of turquoise-colored stone. She looked like a lovely alien princess.

But she was trapped, just like me. Well, not *just* like me. You see, she had wings—long gold-and-yellow ones like a cross between a dragonfly's and a moth's—and they were pinned to a display case as if she were a prized butterfly. The display case was tilted back a bit, like a framed photo on a tabletop, and she was lit by

not one beam of light but three, presumably to better show off the shimmering colors of her wings.

"I mean, get ahold of yourself," she continued, sounding very annoyed. "You're *alive*, aren't you?"

There was a long pause. I had no idea how to respond.

"Yeah," I said finally, wiping the last of the tears

away and glancing at the less fortunate creatures surrounding us.

"Yeah, I . . . I guess I'm lucky, huh?" I continued,
instinctively moving as close to her as I could, which
really only meant going from one side of the glass
dome to the other.

"You can say *that* again," she said, rolling her eyes.

chapter 9

There was another long silence, interrupted only by the crackling of the fire. The girl alien now kept her face turned away from mine, as if she regretted having talked to me in the first place.

"My name is Akiko," I said through the glass.

She didn't react in the slightest. I wasn't sure how well she could hear me.

"My name is Aki—"

"I heard you the first time," she said, her face still turned away from mine. Man, she sure was snooty. But it wasn't like I had a big selection of people to talk to.

"What's *your* name?" I asked.

"Look," she said, facing me at last, "I'm not here to answer your questions, Little Miss Pigtails. So why don't you keep your mouth shut and leave me alone?"

Of all the people to be stuck with! She was just about the most unpleasant person I'd ever met. There was a girl back at Middleton Elementary named Chelsea Worthington who talked to everybody as if they were three grades below her. She even talked to *sixth* graders that way. Well, I didn't think it was possible, but this alien girl was even worse than *her.*

I sat down inside my little glass cell, folded my legs, and propped my head up with both hands. This was going to be a *very* long night.

"Ladmi," I heard the alien say suddenly.

"What?"

"If you must know," she said, still not looking me in the eye, "my name is Ladmi."

"N—" I began, then stopped myself. With someone like her it was hard to know if you were saying the wrong thing—or if it was even *possible* to say the *right* thing. Still, I was dying to find out more about what was going on and what might happen to us and everything else, so I decided to give it a try.

"Nice to meet you, Ladmi."

"Okay, you know my name now," she said, rolling her eyes. "It's not like we're best *buddies* or anything."

The funny thing was, I could tell she wanted to talk to me. She just didn't like to show it. I made a mental note not to take her nastiness personally.

"So how did you get trapped in here?" I asked.

"How does *anyone* get trapped in here?" she responded. I *hate* when people answer a question with another question!

"Well," I said, "I was on a grand tour of the zoo until just a few hours ago. This is supposed to be a vacation for me."

"So what was it, the Tunklefish or the Fillaprims?" she asked with a dark grin.

"Fillaprims!" I said excitedly. "That's right. He said he was going to show us some Fillaprims. . . ."

"*Us?*" she asked, latching on to the word. "Who's 'us'?"

"Me and my friends," I replied. "There are five of us all together: Spuckler, Poog, Mr. Bee—"

"And he only captured *you*?" she interrupted, sounding much more interested than before but also more annoyed. "What makes *you* so special?"

"I—I don't know," I said, considering the question for the first time. Why *had* Yunk separated me from the others? And where *were* the others, anyway? I raised my eyes to the skylight above, silently hoping that they were already on their way to rescue me.

"Well, allow me to answer that question for you, Pigtails," she said, now sounding extremely hostile. "You're *not* special. This is obviously some kind of mistake."

"My name is not Pigtails," I said angrily.

"I don't care what your stupid name is!"

K'CHAK!

A bookshelf on one side of the room suddenly slid sideways and in stepped Norvis Yunk, with Wolo perched on his shoulder. I shut my mouth and remained as still as possible. Ladmi was much more relaxed, but she kept just as quiet as I did.

Yunk had changed into more casual clothes, something like a very fancy bathrobe, and was drinking black liquid from a large bell-shaped goblet. He slid the bookshelf back into place and stepped directly across the room toward me. I was suddenly very thankful for the glass dome, relieved to have a barrier—*any* barrier—between us. To think I'd actually *liked* the guy when I first met him!

He leaned over until his face was just a few inches away from mine. His enormous head was slightly distorted by the curved wall of glass, making his big pock-marked nose look like a bloated pink fish. He stroked his beard and examined me with his round, watery eyes, which were doubly magnified by the glass dome and his own wire-rimmed spectacles.

"She's a good specimen, isn't she, Wolo?" he said gleefully, taking a big swig from his goblet before setting it down on the table. "Not *exactly* what I was hoping for, of course. But as long as I'm barred from entering the Milky Way, we'll just have to make do, I suppose. . . ." He was treating me in an entirely different way now, like a very rare postage stamp or an amoeba under a microscope. The last thing I wanted to do was talk to him, but I couldn't see any way around it.

"Mr. Yunk!" I cried, summoning up the toughest, most defiant-sounding voice I could. "Where are my friends? What have you done with them?"

"I wonder what we should feed her?" Yunk said, talking to Wolo, or perhaps just to himself. Couldn't he hear what I said? Or was he just ignoring me?

"You . . . ," I continued, my voice beginning to tremble with rage, ". . . you can't *do* this to me! King Froptoppit will find out, and then you'll be in trouble. *Big* trouble!" The words didn't sound nearly as threatening as I wanted them to.

"We'll start her off on proteins and starches," he said calmly, "then work our way up to complex sugars. We'll have her grown to maturity in no time at all." It was as if I were no longer human to him, as if the things I'd said to him were no more worthy of a reply than the chattering of a chimpanzee.

Yunk walked over to a nearby cabinet, opened it, and withdrew a shiny tin canister, one of many such containers arranged on several shelves in neat little rows.

He opened the canister, poured a small amount of its contents into one opened hand, and walked back to where I stood. He then stretched out his free hand and placed it on the glass just a few feet above my head. I crouched down as low as I could, afraid that he was going to lift the whole thing up and deprive me of what little protection I had. But instead he merely unscrewed a small round section of glass at the very top of the dome. It was only about eight inches in diameter, just wide enough for him to drop small objects into my little cell. I hungrily inhaled the fresh air that came rushing in, then ducked out of the way as dozens of gray pellets the size of tennis balls rained down on me.

KREET-KREET-KREET!

Yunk screwed the section of glass into place and stood back to watch me eat. I was practically starving at that point, but I didn't want to give him the pleasure of seeing me scarf the stuff down like a wild animal, so I simply stood there and stared back at him.

I had this sudden memory of being at the Middleton Zoo with my mom and dad on a hot summer day about three years ago. I spent the whole day complaining to my parents because it seemed to me that every lion, tiger, and polar bear in the whole dumb place was doing nothing but lying around sleeping. What's the point of going to the zoo if none of the animals *do* anything? In my current circumstances, though, I knew exactly what it was like for those animals: people staring at them, waiting for them to perform. No wonder they didn't do anything.

Yunk eventually shifted his gaze and frowned.

"Perhaps they prefer eating in isolation," he said to Wolo. He waited just a little longer, then turned, picked up his goblet, and went back through the hidden doorway.

K'CHAK-SHHHHH-K'CHOK!

After the bookshelf slid closed, I waited a moment to be sure he was gone for good, then got down on both knees and started eating.

Chapter 10

" 'Perhaps they prefer eating in isolation,'" I said scornfully after finishing the last of the awful chalky pellets, recalling Yunk's words with a shudder. " 'They'? What am I, a *species* or something?"

"Of *course* that's what you are. Don't you get it?"

It was Ladmi. She had removed a small glass comb from a pocket in her dress and was drawing it slowly through her long shimmering hair. She stared off wearily into space, as if talking to me was extremely tiresome and an act of great generosity on her part.

"Well, no, actually. I *don't* get it," I replied, trying not to sound as prissy as she did. "Perhaps you can enlighten me."

"Okay," said Ladmi, "what planet are you from?"

"Earth."

She whipped her head around to face me, her big brown eyes open wide in astonishment.

"You mean you're an *Earthian*?"

"Earth*ling*."

"An Earthian!" she continued, ignoring my correction. "Well, that explains everything."

"No, it doesn't," I insisted. "Not to *me*, anyway."

"Look, Pigtails," she said, evidently unable to address me by any other name, "Yunk has been trying to add an Earthian to this collection for ages. It's been his dream ever since he was a kid."

"What collection?" I asked.

"*This* collection!" she said, waving a hand at all the ghostly glass-domed creatures surrounding us. "Take a good look. This is the largest collection of stuffed humanoids in the universe. Of course, it doesn't hurt that stuffing humanoids is illegal. . . ."

"Wait a minute. You're telling me that I'm part of a collection?"

"Yeeeessss," she said with exaggerated clarity. "Well, you *will* be, anyway, once you're old enough."

"What . . . ," I said, staring at one particularly creepy bug-eyed humanoid on a table just across from me, ". . . what do you mean, 'once you're old enough'?"

"Taxidermy, Pigtails. Taxidermy."

She sure did have a stuck-up way of talking. And the Pigtails bit was *really* getting on my nerves.

"Once you've reached full maturity you're going to end up just like all these other poor saps," she continued, trying to sound casual, "so you might as well get used to the idea."

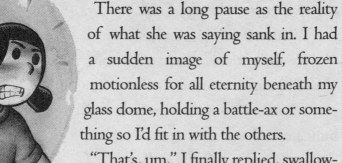

There was a long pause as the reality of what she was saying sank in. I had a sudden image of myself, frozen motionless for all eternity beneath my glass dome, holding a battle-ax or something so I'd fit in with the others.

"That's, um," I finally replied, swallowing hard, "a pretty hard idea to get used to."

"Yeah, well, Yunk's not going to make any exceptions for you," she said, shooting me an accusing glance. "He can't kill *me* because he knows it'll make my wings rot. I'm the one who gets to stay alive, okay? But you . . . well, I hope you like that glass dome, because you're going to be there for a long, long time, Pigtails."

"Stop calling me that!"

"I'll call you whatever I want to!" she snapped back at me. "I didn't ask for a roommate. Things were just fine until you came along. . . ."

"Look," I said, trying very hard not to lose my temper, "I don't know what it is that you think I've done, or what your problem is in general . . ."

She gritted her teeth at the second remark.

". . . but fighting with each other is only going to make things worse. We're in the same boat here—"

"We are *not* the same!" she shouted, straining against her pinned-down wings. "I'm his favorite! You're just some stupid Earthian loser *kid!*"

"All right, that does it," I said, my temper now offi-
cially lost. "I'm not talking to you anymore."

"Finally!" she said with a triumphant shake of her
head. "She actually gets a hint!"

I sat down, turned myself completely away from her,
and . . . well, I guess I just sort of *fumed* for a while.
I'd never met anyone who managed to get me so angry
in such a short time. I was shaking, I was so mad.
Who did she think she was? I hadn't done anything wrong. It was like she *enjoyed* being mean to people, I swear.

At least half an hour went by that way: total silence,
neither of us saying a word. I finally turned my head
just enough to catch sight of her. She had her stupid
little glass comb out again and was busy dolling herself
up for who-knows-what reason.

I sighed, curled up against one side of the dome, and
tried to make myself fall asleep.

It took a very long time.

Chapter 11

The next thing I heard was a muffled scraping noise. It kept getting louder and louder until finally I opened my eyes and sat up to see what was going on. I looked out of my glass cell at Ladmi. She was sound asleep, which was a big relief; the last thing I wanted to do was deal with her again.

As the scraping continued, I became convinced that it was coming from behind the green curtains. The noise suddenly stopped for a minute, then started again, even louder than before. I thought I also heard voices, but I couldn't be sure.

Then:

KRA-THAAAAAASH!

The curtain billowed up into the air, revealing the tangled bodies of none other than Spuckler and Mr. Beeba, who had just tumbled out onto the floor with a mighty thud. Poog floated in after them, narrowly missing the long brass-colored curtain rod, which snapped loose from the wall and dropped squarely onto Mr. Beeba's head.

TLANK!

"YYAAAAARRRRRRRGGGH!"

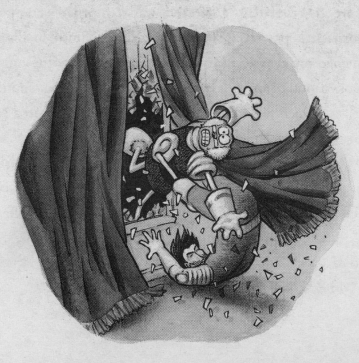

As the curtain slowly collapsed onto the floor, I could see an ornate stained-glass window, which had until now been hidden from view. Or, rather, I could see the *remains* of the window, since Spuckler and Mr. Beeba had just crashed right through it from the outside, leaving little more than a big jagged hole behind them.

"Ya dadburned idjit!" Spuckler cried.

"Shhhhh!" Mr. Beeba warned, apparently thinking it was still possible to conceal their presence despite the deafening racket they'd just made.

I shot a glance at Ladmi. She was wide awake, staring at the clumsy intruders with big fearful eyes.

"Spuckler! Mr. Beeba!" I shouted, pounding on the glass. "Over here!"

They literally jumped for joy when they saw me. Mr. Beeba ran over to my table while Spuckler reached through the window to help bring Gax in from a ledge outside. Gax clicked and whirred as Spuckler placed him on the floor.

"AKIKO!" Gax said, his round body rocking happily back and forth. "THANK GOODNESS WE'VE FOUND YOU!"

Poog floated over to my table and smiled cheerfully through the glass. He gurgled a few syllables in his weird, warbly language. As always, I didn't catch a word, but I figured it was something along the lines of "Long time no see."

"Are you okay? Did he hurt you?" Mr. Beeba asked me.

"Well, I—"

"You *must* accept my apologies, Akiko!" he continued without waiting for my answer. "Mr. Yunk is a very respected zoologist. We had no idea he would turn out to be such a cad!"

"He's pretty creepy, all right," I said, looking down at Mr. Beeba through the glass wall surrounding me. "But he hasn't hurt me. Not yet, anyway."

"Well, well, well," said an all-too-familiar voice, "I take it these are your friends."

It was Ladmi. All heads turned in her direction. She had regained her composure and was combing her hair again, as if the arrival of all these new people was only very slightly interesting to her.

"Yes, Ladmi," I said, wishing I could think of a way to avoid introducing her to everyone.

"Nice t' meetcha, Lad-a-mi," Spuckler said, strolling over to get a better look at her. "I'm Spuckler Boach. Ain't never seen no one like you b'fore. Where ya from?"

"Pleased to meet you, Spuckler," Ladmi replied, speaking much more kindly to him than she ever had to me. "I'm from the planet Zullziban. I take it you've never been there."

"Nope," he replied with grin. "I may have to *now*, though, so as t' getcha back home safe an' sound where ya belong."

No way. Was he offering to rescue her? Maybe I'd misheard him.

"I don't know, Spuckler," Ladmi replied with a sly grin. "Judging by your entrance, I might be safer staying here."

Spuckler chuckled and blushed a little.

It really bothered me that Spuckler and Ladmi were getting along so well. I wanted him to hate her just as much as I did. And the thought of Ladmi's tagging along on *my* rescue party was downright infuriating.

"Miss Ladmi," Mr. Beeba said, stepping over to Spuckler's side, "I assure you that, er, if you should choose to put your faith in us . . . not that you are obligated to do so . . . but if you *were* to . . . that we would have a much easier time exiting . . . than we did, er, entrance-ing."

Entrance-ing? I'd never heard Mr. Beeba speak so awkwardly in the whole time I'd known him. Was he nervous or something?

"I guess I'll just have to take your word for it, Mr. . . ."

"Beeba."

". . . Mr. Beeba. I wonder if I could trouble you or Spuckler to remove some of these pins. It would be ever so nice to move my wings again."

There was nothing I could do but watch as Spuckler and Mr. Beeba fell all over each other trying to assist Ladmi. I'll tell you, the stupid things men do when they see a pretty face and a couple of wings!

A moment later Ladmi was free. She strutted back and forth in front of her display case, showing off her colorful wings like a peacock.

"Whoo doggy, Ladmi," Spuckler said. "Them sure are some purty-lookin' wings ya got there."

They *were* beautiful, I have to admit.

"Yes, Ladmi," Mr. Beeba agreed enthusiastically. "Absolutely gorgeous. You've clearly taken very good care of them—"

"Um, *hello?*" I interrupted, knocking impatiently on the glass. "Remember me? Trapped behind glass. *Not* enjoying it . . ."

"Sorry 'Kiko!" Spuckler said a bit too loudly, as if someone had just snapped him out of a daydream. He leaped up onto my table and began inspecting the glass dome surrounding me.

"Yes, of course, Akiko," Mr. Beeba said, climbing onto my table with some difficulty. "We haven't

89

forgotten you. Just got a little distracted by Ladmi there."

"No, Mr. Beeba. You got *very* distracted by Ladmi there."

"Really, Akiko," Mr. Beeba replied, searching my eyes with a look of mild disbelief. "Surely you don't object to our rescuing Ladmi as well as you."

Did I? You bet I did!

"No," I lied. "I just wish she would be a little more appreciative of all this."

"She's obviously been through quite a lot of hardship, Akiko," said Mr. Beeba. "Have a little compassion for the poor girl."

Chapter 12

It turned out that my glass-dome prison was permanently sealed and that there was no way of freeing me other than cutting through it. Spuckler and Gax started drilling a series of holes in one side of the thing, eventually creating a sort of circular dotted line in the glass. As they worked, Mr. Beeba told the story of how Yunk's guards had imprisoned them in a small room on the other side of the castle shortly after my "disappearance." Spuckler had wanted to fight back, but Mr. Beeba had convinced him that allowing themselves to be locked up would give them a better chance of rescuing me later on.

"I still think I shoulda popped 'em all a good one right in th' jaw," Spuckler said, sounding as if it had been one of his life's biggest missed opportunities.

"Ahem," Mr. Beeba continued. "In any case, we all owe a great debt of gratitude to Poog. He was the one who provided our means of escape. He recited an ancient incantation which caused the door of our cell to levitate off its hinges. A most impressive sight, I assure you."

Poog beamed.

"Gotta learn me one of them there magical spells," said Spuckler as he drilled another hole, "an' when I do, you're gonna see all *kinds* of things levitate. . . ."

Mr. Beeba rolled his eyes. "To make a long story short," he concluded, "Poog was then able to discern your whereabouts and guide us here to this window."

"Thanks, Poog," I said through the glass as Spuckler and Gax drilled the last of the holes. "You've saved our lives so many times now I'm starting to lose count."

Poog blinked his big shiny eyes and smiled modestly. Pounding just once with a single clenched fist, Spuckler popped the circle of glass out, instantly creating my means of escape. Taking his hand, I crawled through the passageway as quickly as I could and jumped out onto the surface of the table. As I did, there was a loud clicking noise and Spuckler looked in horror at the polished-wood floor of the empty glass dome: It had just raised itself by an inch or two.

"Dang!" he said. "Shoulda known it was weight sensitive."

"W-weight sensitive?" Mr. Beeba asked.

BOO-WEEEP! BOO-WEEP! BOO-WEEEP! BOO-WEEP!

Suddenly a deafeningly loud alarm pierced the air at regular intervals, echoing off the walls and causing us all to clamp our hands tightly over our ears.

"No!" Ladmi cried. "Yunk's going to be in here within seconds!"

What happened next is kind of a blur to me now. Everything took place so fast; there simply wasn't time to think things over. Spuckler led all of us, Ladmi included, back to the window, and one by one we crawled onto the ledge outside. We were at least a hundred feet above the ground, and the view was absolutely terrifying. The ledge we were on was a series of two-foot-wide slabs of stone, big enough to crawl along but still narrow enough to fall off if you weren't careful.

"Now, Akiko . . . ," Mr. Beeba began.

"I know, I know!" I said. "Don't look down!"

"Yes. Quite."

The *boo-weeep-boo-weeep*ing of the alarm grew fainter as we all crawled along the ledge. A dull orange sun was just beginning to creep up over the trees of Yunk's estate. The air was damp and chilly. From somewhere in the distance came the roars and howls of alien animals as the Intergalactic Zoo woke up to another morning. I shuddered as I remembered how much we'd all been enjoying ourselves just a day ago, before we had any idea of the danger we were getting ourselves into.

Spuckler led the way to a corner of the building where the bricks jutted out every foot or so. It wasn't exactly a stepladder or anything, but it certainly offered the quickest way of getting to the roof. Poog floated up first to check things out. I watched as his round purple body disappeared over the edge of the roof, then reappeared a few seconds later; he evidently

hadn't found anything for us to worry about. Mr. Beeba and I went first, followed by Ladmi. Spuckler and Gax brought up the rear, coating the bricks behind us with a layer of slippery oil to slow down any would-be followers.

Arriving on the roof created a temporary feeling of safety. The sun was now mostly above the trees, warming the air considerably, and the songs of birds were somehow reassuring, even if they didn't entirely drown out the noise of the alarm still echoing from below. If not for our current predicament I'm sure we'd have all agreed that it was a perfectly lovely morning.

Spuckler led us up the orange-tiled roof to an alcove tucked between two towers. A flock of yellow-feathered birds that apparently made its home in this very spot screeched noisily and took to the sky with a flurry of flapping wings. Mr. Beeba almost lost his footing once, sending a chipped tile skipping down the roof and making us wonder if he hadn't just given away our location to someone below. We scurried into the shadows provided by the tower walls and prayed no one would find us.

Chapter 13

We didn't get much time to rest.

A window opened just a few feet above us and out popped a small orange-and-green-capped head. Wolo!

"Nuglug wup-lup!" he shouted angrily, pointing at us with a quivering outstretched paw. *"Zid-lib zid-lib! Mup mup mup!"*

Now we were really finished!

But then:

"Nodwud lep-lep!"

It was Ladmi. She was talking back to Wolo in his own language!

"*Oglug Wolo,*" she continued with a desperate look in her eyes. "*Ludlip Wolo!*"

"*Zod zod zod zod zod . . . ,*" Wolo replied, shaking his head vigorously.

"*Ludlip ludlip Wolo,*" Ladmi pleaded. "*Pupnip pupnip. Yunk no nell-nuk . . .*"

Wolo narrowed his eyes. He looked as if he was weighing Ladmi's words very carefully, as if she had made him an offer that was very difficult to refuse.

"*Ludlip Wolo, ludlip—*" Ladmi began again.

"*Zod!*" Wolo interrupted. He made several loud clicking noises with his teeth, then: "*Zod! Zod! Zod!*"

And with that he disappeared.

Suddenly Ladmi was once again the center of attention. She faced a barrage of questions from Spuckler and Mr. Beeba while Gax and Poog looked on approvingly. Ladmi explained that during her many months of captivity she had befriended Wolo and had learned his language bit by bit.

"Good work, Ladmi!" Mr. Beeba said with a look of great admiration. "This is going to be quite an asset to our cause. I'm a bit of a linguist myself, you know—"

"So whadja say to him?" Spuckler interrupted impatiently. "Is he gonna rat on us?"

"I . . . I'm afraid so," Ladmi answered. "He's too scared of Yunk. Too scared of what Yunk might do to him. I tried to get him to escape along with us, but he refused."

"Don't be too hard on yourself, Ladmi," Mr. Beeba said, laying one of his oversized hands on her head. "I'm sure you did your best."

Watching Mr. Beeba and Spuckler, I suddenly had an awful feeling. It was as if they were becoming better friends with Ladmi than they were with me. I guess it was pretty stupid of me to be worrying about something like that when all of our lives were in danger, but I couldn't help myself. The more I thought about it, the more convinced I became that they really did like her more than me. And who could blame them? She was certainly prettier than me. And smarter, too. The only thing I seemed to be good for lately was getting us all in trouble. After all, if I hadn't told Norvis Yunk that I was from the planet Earth . . .

"All right," Spuckler said, putting one hand on Ladmi's shoulder and the other on Mr. Beeba's, "I got a plan. Gax, I need you to sneak down from this here rooftop and find us some transportation."

"TRANSPORTATION, SIR? BUT—"

"No buts!" Spuckler snapped back at him. "We need to get th' heck off this planet, and we ain't gonna do it by jus' flappin' our arms."

Gax shook a bit and made a nervous ticking sound with his neck.

"Now come on, Gax," Spuckler continued. "We been through worse scrapes than this an' come out fine in the end. You go get us a ship—*any* ship—and high-tail it back here just as fast as y' can."

"Y-YES, SIR," Gax answered, straightening himself up as best he could.

"Tha's my boy," Spuckler said, rubbing Gax's helmet proudly. "Now go on. Get outta here."

We all watched in silence as Gax rolled down the gentle slope of the roof, his metallic surface glinting a bit in the morning sunlight. He quietly unfolded a few suction-cupped legs from within his body, used them to position himself vertically on one of the tower walls, and began his descent to the ground. A moment later he was gone.

"We've got to go somewhere else," Ladmi said, rising to her feet. "Once Wolo tells Yunk where we are, they'll both come straight here to recapture us."

We all rose and followed Ladmi across the rooftop, up another wall, and past twisting brick chimneys and towering black air vents. By now my mood had gone from bad to worse. I deliberately moved to the back of the group, allowing myself to fall behind. I think I was kind of testing them, trying to see if they even noticed I was still there. There's only one problem when you test friends like that: They hardly ever pass the test. Before long I was separated from them by more than twenty feet and they still hadn't even turned around to check on me. Didn't they *care* about me *at all*?

These were the thoughts going through my head when suddenly my right foot slid out from underneath me. I struggled for a terrible second or two to regain my balance, but it was no use. All at once I completely lost my footing and tumbled headlong down the rooftop!

Chapter 14

After a dizzying number of backflips, sideflips, and just plain old head-over-heels somersaults, I found myself hanging by my fingertips from a loose gutter at the very edge of the roof. I was covered from head to toe with dust, dirt, and—try not to think about this too much, okay?—foul-smelling green stuff that must have been the droppings of those yellow-feathered birds I'd seen earlier.

"Spuckler!" I cried as loudly as I could. "Mr. Beeba!"

I allowed myself one quick glimpse down to see just how high I was above the ground. Luckily just fifteen feet or so below me I could see a second rooftop, the very one we'd been camped on a moment before. If

I fell, I might get off with just a sprained ankle. But I didn't plan on falling.

"Poog!" I called out.

No response.

I thought about calling out Ladmi's name. *Thought* about it.

"It's all right," I told myself. "They'll notice I'm missing and come back here looking for me."

My arms were starting to get weak from the strain. I tried inching my way up the loose gutter to a section that was more firmly attached to the roof. Each move produced a groan of protest from the gutter, as if it were warning me not to push my luck. Then, in the middle of all this:

"Pud-lug?"

It was the voice of Norvis Yunk. His head was just a few yards below my dangling feet, poking out from the very same window Wolo's head had emerged from just a few minutes before.

"Zod, Wolo," Yunk continued. *"Mum-zuk pud-lug."*

I remained as still as I could. The wind blew hard against me, though, causing the gutter to groan noisily.

Yunk stuck his head farther out, shielded his eyes with one hand, and turned his face up in my direction.

He saw me.

There was an awful silent second or two during which Yunk simply stared at me in disbelief. Then he went red in the face and began trembling with rage.

"*Grog-not, Wolo!*" he shouted. "*Grog-not!*"

I didn't have time to think about what to do. My body just went into action. I swung myself back and forth once . . .

. . . twice . . .

. . . then flipped myself back up to the rooftop like a kid showing off on a playground jungle gym. I wish someone could have seen me. I'll bet it looked pretty cool.

Without looking back, I tried to make for the top of the roof, but before I got even a few feet I was yanked back by one of Wolo's three-fingered paws, closed fast around my left ankle. I spun my head back and caught one terrifying glimpse of the look on his face: his beady black eyes squeezed into an angry squint, his beaklike lips drawn back around sharp white teeth.

I raised my right knee as high as I could, then released it with all the force I could muster. I didn't see—but definitely felt—my sneakered foot smack right into his face. I turned my head just in time to see his long furry tail disappear over the edge of the roof.

Yes!

I scrambled back up to the top of the roof. There on the other side of one of the roof's ridges were Spuckler, Ladmi, Mr. Beeba, and Poog. They were combing the area, looking for me in the completely wrong place.

"'Kiko!" Spuckler shouted when he saw me. "Where ya been? Ya had us scared half t' death!"

My head was a whirl of mixed emotions. I was terrified by the knowledge that Wolo and Norvis Yunk were coming after us at that very moment and angry with Spuckler and the others for having totally failed my little test. Basically I was a wreck.

"C'mon, 'Kiko," Spuckler said as he grabbed me by the arm (a little too roughly, I thought) and pulled me along to join the others. "Ladmi's going to show us a safer place to hide out for a while."

Ladmi, Ladmi, Ladmi. Why couldn't she have already been stuffed and mounted on the wall by the time I met up with her?

"Are you all right, Pigtails?" Ladmi asked with a wink. "Looks like you need a shower. . . ."

"Pigtails!" Beeba repeated with a stifled chuckle.

I glared at him and he grimaced apologetically.

"So what were ya doin' over there, anyway?" Spuckler asked as we all began scaling the roof to an even higher elevation. "Sightseein'?"

Did he really expect me to laugh at a stupid joke like that?

"I . . . I had to tie my shoe."

Spuckler and Mr. Beeba both shot me a disbelieving glance but let my answer stand. Poog stared at me too, his big glassy eyes focused on me with great concern.

Why didn't I tell them the truth? That I'd given away our location and that Yunk and Wolo were hot on our heels? I don't know. Any way you look at it, lying was just going to make things worse. I guess I thought I was punishing them. They *needed* to be punished. I really believed that right then.

"Just up here," Ladmi called back from the head of our little group, "there's an area where I don't think anyone can get to us. Wolo used to tell me about it. It's where he goes when he doesn't want Yunk to find him."

When she reached the top, she came to a halt. One by one we joined her, each of us stopping at the exact same spot. There, across a thirty-foot-wide horizontal surface just beyond where we stood, were Norvis Yunk and Wolo. And they weren't alone.

Chapter 15

Hovering just behind Yunk's head was a swarm of oversized insect creatures—humming, buzzing things that looked like they had been crossbred from hornets and porcupines. They were about a foot long from head to tail, with a mass of beady green eyes on either side of their nasty little heads. Hundreds of short black needles covered the surface of their bodies, and they hovered in the air with the precision of miniature helicopters. How many of them were there? I don't know. Thirty. Forty. Maybe more.

"Nizziks," Ladmi whispered, her face filled with dread. "The needles are filled with Somnus-Ether. More than three stings and you're out cold."

I looked quickly to see everyone's reactions. Spuckler appeared stoic as always. Mr. Beeba seemed petrified as always. But Poog . . . It was the first time I'd ever seen him look scared. He was practically shaking. Could these Nizziks actually hurt him somehow?

Yunk had an extremely odd expression on his face. He didn't look angry, exactly. He actually seemed a little worried. Not for himself, of course. I think he was concerned about Ladmi and me, but in a slightly cold way. Like a mother might worry about her favorite porcelain figurine or a father about the finish on his brand-new car. His eyes kept darting back and forth: Ladmi, me, Ladmi, me. He must have been trying to figure out how to get us back without damaging us.

He opened his mouth, gritted his teeth, and made a few short buzzing noises.

"*Thuzzzzz. Kzz-fzzz. Kzz-fzzz.*"

One of the Nizziks flew forward.

Was he actually able to talk to these things?

"*Fzz-nkk. Pzzz. Thuzzz-thuzz.*"

Yunk was pointing directly at Spuckler, Mr. Beeba, and Poog, carefully avoiding Ladmi and me.

"All right, Yunkster . . . ," Spuckler began, preparing to deliver one of his fearless ultimatums. He never got the chance.

"Thuh-YUZZZZZ!"

Norvis shouted these last words as loudly as he could. The Nizziks immediately rushed forward, covering the distance to us in less than a second. I instinctively dropped to my knees and buried my head in my arms. My eyes were shut tight, so I couldn't see a thing. But my ears! They were filled with the most horrid sound I'd ever heard: a buzzing so loud it was like thousands of tiny screams layered one on top of the other. I tried plugging my ears, but that hardly muffled the noise at all. I kept thinking that I'd soon be covered by the hideous creatures, but they never even touched me. After an awful half-minute of this I finally raised my head and opened my eyes.

There was such a scene of confusion that it took me a while to see who was where and what was what. Somewhere amid the black cloud of Nizziks darting this way and that I made out the red-suited torso of Spuckler, his arms flailing about, trying to fend off the attack. And there, crouching between Spuckler's knees . . . was that Mr. Beeba? I located Ladmi a yard or two to my left, but I couldn't see Poog anywhere. I still had a vivid image in my mind of his frightened expression before the attack. The thought of anything bad happening to Poog was enough to make me want to cry.

"Here, take this."

It was Ladmi. She was handing me a long, sharp shard of stone that she had created by breaking one of the roof tiles into pieces.

"You've got to stab them," she said.

"S-stab them?"

"Don't worry. The Nizziks won't attack you and me. Yunk doesn't want to damage our skins."

"But—"

"*Stab* them, Akiko," she said, laying her hand on mine and closing my fingers around the piece of stone. "You can do it. They're very thin-skinned."

And with that she rose to her feet and began striking back against the Nizziks, missing them entirely most of the time but occasionally striking one dead-on, sending it spiraling off the roof like a downed fighter jet.

I was vaguely aware that Ladmi had just called me Akiko for the first time.

Clenching the shard of stone in my hand, I jumped

to my feet.

It wasn't pretty, let me tell you that. I must have sliced that crude little weapon through the air more than a hundred times a minute. It took me dozens of tries before I managed to do anything other than make my arm sore, but when I struck my first Nizzik, I found that Ladmi was absolutely right: They *were* thin-skinned. *Very* thin-skinned.

As Ladmi and I continued our counterattack, Norvis Yunk shouted ever more frantic instructions to his troops.

"Bzzz-whik! BZZZ-WHIIIK!"

The Nizziks pressed onward against Spuckler and Mr. Beeba. There was still no sign of Poog, which was really starting to frighten me.

After a while it became clear that Ladmi and I were making progress. The bodies of Nizziks lay strewn about the rooftop, and the dozen or so that remained were flying in very tight circles around Spuckler and Mr. Beeba, some of them latched directly on to their bodies. Ladmi and I joined forces at this point, positioning ourselves on either side of Spuckler, taking care to stab only the Nizziks and not our friends struggling valiantly beneath them.

The horrid buzzing-screaming noise had decreased to a low, murmuring hum. After a while I was able to count the number of Nizziks left alive. Five. Then two. Then none.

Ladmi and I stood there, weapons in hand, panting. Spuckler was on his feet but was clearly dazed. Mr. Beeba was not so lucky. He was flat on his back, entirely unconscious. I looked around for Poog but still couldn't see him.

That's when I heard a faint buzzing sound somewhere very high above our heads. I craned my neck and looked up into the cool blue of the morning sky.

Poog was hundreds of feet above us, three Nizziks making slow deliberate circles around him. Every once in a while there was a split-second white-hot flash of light—a defensive weapon of Poog's?—and the number of Nizziks was reduced by one.

"That's right, Poog!" I shouted with a smile. "Get 'em! Get those little monsters!"

And he did.

Eventually.

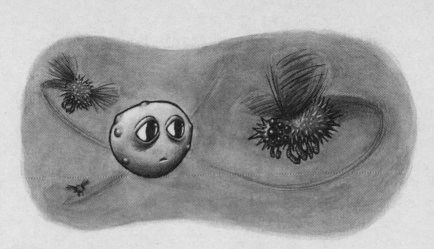

It took longer than I expected.

When Poog was done with his tormentors, he glided down toward me, a bit unsteadily, I thought. As he approached, I saw to my great horror that he had not made it through the attack unscathed. His until-now-perfect purple skin was covered with little bluish welts, and his eyes were more than half closed. He gave me a weak smile and continued to descend until he was right at the level of my ankles, his body nearly touching the roof. Then it *did* touch the roof. This was the first time I'd ever seen Poog fail to defy gravity, and if someone had jumped up and slapped me hard on the face, they couldn't have stunned me more than Poog did at that moment. Tears came to my eyes as I stared at the ghastly scene of Poog at my feet, his face raised toward mine, his eyelids slowly closing over his glassy black eyes. Another few seconds and Poog, like Mr. Beeba, was unconscious.

Chapter 16

Was Poog okay? Had the Nizzik stings permanently damaged him somehow? Would they prove fatal? This last question was so frightening, I immediately wished it hadn't occurred to me. I wiped the tears from my eyes and tried to push the thought from my mind.

I glared angrily at Norvis Yunk, who was still standing across from us with Wolo at his side. He had one hand propped on his side and was stroking his chin with the other. Clearly he had not planned on Spuckler's coming out of the attack still standing and was now having to come up with a way to deal with him.

Ladmi and I stayed at Spuckler's side. He still looked dazed, as if it was all he could do to remain on his feet.

"I can't believe you're still awake," Ladmi said to him. "You've got more than a dozen stings on your face alone."

Spuckler grinned, trying hard to be his usual boastful self.

"Ah, thad ain' nothin', La'mi," he said, his words now slurred much more than usual. "Bring on s'more a them Nizziks. I can take 'em. . . . I'll eat 'em for breakfiss, tha's whad I'll do. . . ."

The wind whistled across the rooftop, ruffling the wings of the Nizziks, most of which now lay belly-up, their spindly black legs twitching weakly in the air. I tried not to look at Mr. Beeba and Poog. Seeing them as they were at the moment was just too much to take.

Spuckler was facing Yunk now, blinking over and over, as if staying alert required an enormous effort. Yunk had removed a large crossbow-like weapon from a holster at his side and was loading it with little red darts.

"Tranquilizer darts," Ladmi explained. "We've got to make a run for it. It's our only chance."

"C'mon, Spuckler," I said, grabbing him firmly by the arm. "We have to go now."

"Naw, 'Kiko," Spuckler answered, "you know me better 'n that. No runnin'."

Yunk had finished loading his weapon and was now aiming it squarely at Spuckler's chest.

"No!" Ladmi and I shouted as we leaped in front of Spuckler. We were both betting that Yunk wouldn't want to hurt us, his valuable collectibles. And we were right. In an instant we had become highly effective living shields.

Yunk grunted angrily as he began circling us, trying to get a clear shot at Spuckler. Ladmi and I moved into the line of fire at every turn. Once or twice he nearly took a shot, but he evidently considered it too risky. Wolo chattered nervously on the sidelines.

The stalemate could have gone on for hours if not for the impatience of Spuckler. He had apparently decided to risk everything in a desperate bid to take Yunk down.

Pushing Ladmi and me roughly aside, Spuckler lurched forward and hurled himself at Norvis Yunk. I caught one brief glimpse of Yunk's horrified expression before the two of them rolled behind a towering black chimney and out of sight. My heart jumped into my throat. Ladmi and I ran after them. The next thing I saw was Yunk flat on his back at the very edge of the rooftop. Spuckler, his back to us, stood triumphantly above him. Yes! Spuckler had beaten him!

THUK!

Spuckler doubled over, his hands on his stomach, and suddenly collapsed. Norvis Yunk rose to a sitting position and smiled, proudly holding his crossbow in one hand.

Spuckler was out cold.

Ladmi and I gave each other a panicked look. It was just the two of us now, with no one left to defend us. Yunk was already back on his feet, climbing up to the spot where we stood.

"Come on, Akiko," Ladmi said. "We've got to make a run for it. We'll find a hiding place somewhere here on the roof."

I looked at Ladmi, at Yunk, and finally at Mr. Beeba, Poog, and Spuckler, still lying unconscious. I turned back to Ladmi and shook my head slowly.

She stared at me as if I'd completely lost my mind. And maybe I had. But when Norvis Yunk arrived at the spot where we stood, running away was the furthest thing from my mind.

Chapter 17

"It's over, little Akiko," Norvis Yunk said calmly, confidently. Those were the first words he'd said to me in a long, long time. He tossed the crossbow back to Wolo, who caught it and twirled it with one hand like a show-off cowboy.

"Come," Norvis said with a gentle smile, extending his hand to me as if he expected me to go with him quietly. "Let's get you and Ladmi back where you belong, before"—he broke off, inspecting my arms and cheeks with cold, squinty eyes—"before something gets damaged."

"No!" I said. "I'm not an animal in your zoo,

and I'm not a part of your nasty little collection, either!"

He stared at me with a blank expression, as if he wasn't really listening to me but was only planning his next move.

"I'm sorry you feel that way, Akiko," he said. "I know for a fact that Ladmi here feels quite differently."

I shot a glance at Ladmi. She had a very uncomfortable look on her face.

"Isn't that right, Ladmi?" Yunk asked knowingly. "You're my prized possession, the jewel of my trophy room. No one else gives you all the care and attention that I do. No one ever has or ever will. In my world you're special, as special as they come. Surely you don't want to go back to being just another girl from Zullziban."

I stared in amazement at Ladmi. She was actually thinking it over.

"Ladmi, are you crazy?" I cried, grabbing her by the arm. "We can't give up without a fight!"

"He's right, Akiko," she said, her self-confidence seeming to evaporate right before my eyes. "I *am* special here. . . ."

"You're *trapped* here, Ladmi, that's all," I told her, tightening my grip on her arm. "And you don't need a creep like Yunk to make you feel special."

"But—"

Suddenly Yunk lurched forward and grabbed me around the waist.

"Gotcha!"

There was no time to think. Only to react.

I reached up and clamped my fingers around Yunk's neck, doing my best to choke him. He was so much bigger than me, it was like trying to wrap my fingers around a giant sack of flour. I didn't have a prayer of doing him any real harm, but I didn't care. I squeezed his neck as hard as I could.

He chuckled.

I felt his enormous fingers close more securely around my waist. His hands were so big, he could hold me pretty comfortably that way and still have one hand free. I strained to press my fingers harder, but it seemed to have no effect on him. I caught a glimpse of his other hand. He was clutching a damp cloth that stank of that same awful chemical stuff he'd used to knock me out before.

"Give in, child," he said. "Don't hurt yourself."

Suddenly I saw Ladmi fluttering nearby. Was she going to help me? I couldn't tell.

All at once she grabbed hold of Yunk's free hand, locked her teeth on it, and bit down as hard as she could.

"Aaayygh!"

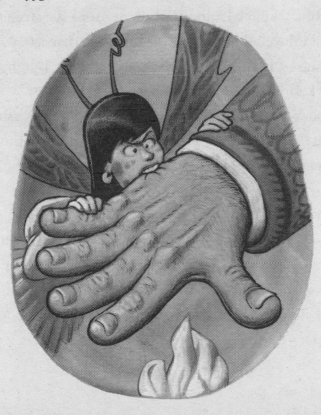

Yunk winced as he dropped the chemical-soaked cloth, letting it fall to the rooftop. In a flash Ladmi swooped down and snatched it up. Within seconds she had the cloth firmly clamped over Yunk's nose and mouth. The chemicals started taking effect almost immediately. Yunk let go of me and began grasping at Ladmi with frantic swipes of his big red fingers, spinning his entire body in circles.

"Run, Akiko!" Ladmi shouted at me as she struggled to hold the cloth in place. "This is your chance!"

I stayed right where I was. No way was I going to leave Ladmi alone with this guy.

I shot a glance at Wolo. He stood with the crossbow in his hands, watching Yunk go around and around, taking aim, stopping, taking aim, stopping. Once he got a clear shot at Ladmi, I figured it would all be over.

I threw my arms around one of Yunk's knees and locked my legs around the other, turning myself into a pair of human handcuffs. Sure enough, Yunk lost his footing and fell headlong onto his face. Ladmi narrowly avoided being crushed as he hit the surface of the roof and started rolling.

All was a blur as the three of us somersaulted down the steep incline of the roof. Yunk reached out and grabbed hold of a little stone gargoyle that was jutting out from the edge of the roof, halting our fall and leaving all three of us swaying precariously in midair.

I was hanging at the very bottom, still holding on to Yunk's leg with all the strength my arms had left. Staring down from where I clung, I could see the glass of the trophy-room skylight twenty or thirty feet below. If Yunk lost his grip, all three of us would go crashing right back into the room we'd just come from, probably getting ourselves a couple of nice broken bones in the process.

That's when I felt Ladmi's arms fold themselves quite comfortably around my chest. She had let go of Yunk, fluttered over with her big beautiful wings, and placed herself right up against my back.

"Let go already, will you, Pigtails?" she whispered in my ear. "I've carried heavier stuff than *you* with these wings, trust me."

I did as I was told. Ladmi carried me up and out of harm's way, depositing me gently back on the roof, safely out of Yunk's reach.

Yunk, it was plain to see, was struggling with the weight of his own enormous body and with the continuing effects of the chemicals he'd inhaled. It was all he could do just to keep his grip on the little stone gargoyle. There was a moment there when I thought we ought to try to help him in spite of everything he'd done to us. He looked so pathetic.

Then, with one violent heave of his body, he hoisted himself up until both of his elbows were propped on the edge of the roof. Ladmi and I instinctively backed farther away, but with Wolo standing guard behind us there was nowhere left to run.

Another heave and Yunk had a knee up on the roof. One last heave and he had saved himself.

"Come back here!" he shouted as he crawled up the roof toward us. He looked angry, *really* angry, for the first time.

"You can't get away from me!" he cried. "You're *mine*, do you hear me? *Mine!*"

THUK!

Suddenly, as if by magic, a single bright red dart appeared right in the middle of Yunk's left shoulder.

He groaned in pain as he began to slip back down to the edge of the roof.

I spun my head around to see none other than Wolo, standing a good thirty feet behind us, the crossbow held confidently with both paws. It was pointed directly at his master.

Yunk gave out an anguished cry as he lost his grip and dropped over the edge of the roof.

A long second of silence followed. Then:

PRAA-KAAAAASH!

The sound of shattering glass echoed across the rooftop. Ladmi and I dashed forward, feeling certain that we no longer had anything to fear from Yunk but somehow needing to see it for ourselves. There he lay far below us, encircled by the jagged hole he had just made in the skylight, facedown on the carpeted floor. His legs twitched once or twice. Then he fell into a deep, deep sleep, becoming nearly as motionless as all the ghastly stuffed creatures that surrounded him.

Chapter 18

Ladmi and I ran back up the roof to check on
Spuckler, Mr. Beeba, and Poog. They were all still
asleep but breathing steadily. They actually looked
quite peaceful, and part of me wished I could join
them right then and there for a nice long nap.

"Wolo!" Ladmi cried out, calling him to our side.
"Ib-zizz mimbaa. Nin-wik nin-wik?"

A brief conversation in Wolo's language followed,
during which Ladmi visibly relaxed. The two of them
talked like old friends.

"They'll be okay," Ladmi translated after a moment.
"They may stay asleep for a few more hours, though."

Ladmi, Wolo, and I sat together and talked as we waited for the others to wake up. I thanked Wolo for saving us and apologized for having kicked him earlier. Ladmi said she wasn't the least bit surprised that Wolo had switched sides. She said she'd always known that Wolo had a good heart.

"Speaking of switching sides," I said to Ladmi, "I'm sure glad you weren't persuaded by all that 'I make you feel special' stuff Yunk was saying."

There was a pause as she seemed to gather her thoughts.

"It's funny," she replied at last. "I was so used to being Yunk's prized possession, I guess I thought it was the only thing I was good for. I mean, it's nice to have someone admiring you every day, telling you how beautiful and rare you are. It may sound strange, but I'm going to miss being the center of attention."

"Trust me, Ladmi," I told her. "*That* kind of attention you can do without."

"Can I?" she asked.

"Look, Ladmi," I said. "You and I deserve much more than a spotlight in some creepy old zookeeper's collection. We've got our whole lives ahead of us. And who cares whether people think we're special, anyway? We *are* special. That's just all there is to it."

"Thanks, Pigtails," she said. "I wish I could look at things the way you do."

"So do I," I replied with a grin. "I have a bad habit of not following my own advice."

Ladmi laughed, and I laughed right along with her. It was hard to believe that only an hour or so earlier I had hated her more than almost anyone I'd ever met. Now she seemed like a good friend of mine, someone it would be hard to say goodbye to. (Okay, she *had* gone back to calling me Pigtails again, but hey, nobody's perfect.)

Mr. Beeba was the first to wake up. Then Poog. And finally, after another hour, Spuckler. They were a little groggy at first but returned to their normal selves soon enough. I thanked them all for risking their lives to save me. I was especially concerned about Poog, but Mr. Beeba assured me that he was okay, just a little dazed from the Nizzik venom. It was indeed one of the few poisons in the universe that Poog was not immune to.

Ladmi and I told Spuckler, Mr. Beeba, and Poog the story of how we'd escaped from the clutches of Norvis Yunk, drawing admiring looks from all three of them. Wolo stood by Ladmi's side, smiling happily when we got to the part where he saved the day.

We had gone through the entire story two times and were beginning on a third when Gax returned with our "borrowed" transportation. It was a big gray boxy spaceship, something like a freight car with rockets in the back. Evidently it was designed for carrying animals to and from the zoo.

Spuckler beamed.

"That's my 'bot!" he said, opening a hatch near the front of the ship and patting Gax on the helmet. "Now come on, gang. We best move on before ol' Yunk snaps out of it. That feller puts up a heckuva fight." He paused, then added, "Almos' as stubborn as *me*, come t' think of it. . . ."

We all piled into the back of the ship, Wolo included. The large, airy compartment was piled high with a grassy blue substance that smelled like a mix between straw and several different varieties of stinky alien manure. (Just what I needed: more alien droppings.)

There was a rumbling, roaring sound as Spuckler revved the engines. The whole ship rattled and shook, then began rising into the air at an incredible speed. The force of it pressed all of us hard against the floor, which vibrated so intensely it made my fingers numb. Gradually both the noise and the vibrating eased a bit. Through several small portals on the walls we saw the blue sky of Quilk fade into the star-filled depths of outer space. My whole body seemed to sigh as we left the Intergalactic Zoo behind us, never to return again.

Spuckler slid a window open in the front of the compartment so he could pop his head through and talk to us.

"Now, Ladmi," he said, "whaddya say we take you on home to Zullziban? I reckon you ain't been there in a while."

"You're right about that," she said with a smile.

"An' what about Wolo? Where we gonna take him?"

"Oh, he's coming with me," Ladmi replied, stroking Wolo's head gently with one hand. Wolo made a happy purring noise like an oversized cat.

I leaned back into a big fluffy pile of the blue straw stuff and folded my hands behind my head. I figured I'd just rest my eyes for a few minutes, but as it turned out I fell almost immediately into a long, deep, dreamless sleep.

Chapter 19

I **awoke** feeling very disoriented. I rubbed the sleep out of my eyes and took in my surroundings: the gray interior walls of the ship, the piles of blue straw. Mr. Beeba was sitting on my left and Gax on my right. Poog was floating in front of me, looking much happier and healthier than he had only a few hours before. Everyone looked better—everyone except . . .

"Ladmi! Wolo!" I said, looking anxiously around for them. "Where are they?"

"I'm sorry, Akiko," Mr. Beeba explained. "Ladmi asked us not to wake you."

"Not to . . . You mean . . ."

"I'm afraid so, Akiko. We dropped them off on the planet Zullziban just over an hour ago. Ladmi said she hated sad farewells."

"Sad farewells?" I repeated, surprised at how upset I was by her absence. "She was sad to say goodbye to me?"

"VERY MUCH SO, MA'AM," Gax answered. "SHE SEEMED TO HAVE GROWN QUITE ATTACHED TO YOU DURING THE BRIEF TIME YOU SPENT TOGETHER. SHE WANTED YOU TO HAVE THIS."

A thin mechanical arm popped out of Gax's body, displaying a delicate silver necklace with a bright turquoise-colored stone as its centerpiece: Ladmi's necklace.

"Real purty, ain't it?" Spuckler called back from the front of the ship. "That's Nootstone, ya know. Hard t' come by these days."

"She said it would bring you luck," Mr. Beeba explained. "Not that I, as a man of science, put much credence in the concept of jewelry bestowing good fortune. It doesn't really hold up if you look at it from a *molecular* standpoint. . . ."

"Oh, just hush, Mr. Beeba," I said, drawing both ends of the necklace up behind my neck, "and help me put this thing on."

As we made our way back to Earth, I asked Mr. Beeba question after question about Ladmi. Unfortunately, he wasn't able to answer very many of them. Ladmi had said goodbye without explaining where she had come from or where she was going. He said she'd looked happy to be free again, though, and so had Wolo.

"There she is, dead ahead!" Spuckler announced loudly. "Earth!"

I stood up and poked my head through the window

at the front of the compartment. Sure enough, there beyond the ship's dusty windshield was that old familiar blue-green ball, growing steadily larger as we zoomed in closer and closer. It sure was nice to see it again.

"Don't take this the wrong way, guys," I said, "but next time King Froptoppit wants to send me on a vacation, tell him I'd rather stay home."

Mr. Beeba smiled apologetically and—for once—said nothing.

Chapter 20

It was late morning when Spuckler brought the ship down for a landing in a park nearby Middleton Elementary. I was really scared someone would see the ship, but I'm pretty sure no one did, since we were surrounded by trees and thick bushes. Spuckler hopped out and opened the back doors, allowing me to step back onto Earth. Had we really only been gone for one day? If so, it was the longest day of my life, that's for sure.

Mr. Beeba used a little blue-and-yellow remote-control box to contact the Akiko replacement robot. He pushed a few buttons and put the box to his ear.

"She'll be here soon," he explained after a moment. "She's in the middle of a pop quiz in your history class."

"Tell her to take her time," I said. "Those pop quizzes are tough."

Ten or fifteen minutes later the Akiko robot appeared, my book bag slung over her shoulder. As always she looked exactly like me, except this time she was wearing a little pink-and-orange friendship bracelet.

"Denise Montoure made this for me," she explained, "after I helped her with a book report."

"No way!" I replied. "I'm friends with Denise Montoure now? I thought she hated me."

"Not anymore," the Akiko robot said as she took the little handmade bracelet off and tied it around my wrist. "Of course you'll probably have to keep helping out with her book reports. . . ."

"Oh, great," I replied. "Well, it could have been worse. At least you didn't make friends with Chelsea Worthington."

"Better hurry," she said with a wink. "You're already late for gym class."

I wish I hadn't had to say goodbye to everyone so quickly. I hugged Poog first, then Spuckler, and finally Mr. Beeba and Gax. (Actually I had trouble figuring out how to hug Gax, so I just kind of gave him a little kiss on the helmet.) Finally I hugged the Akiko robot, who advised me to take Ladmi's necklace off and keep it in my pocket. Good thing she pointed that out. I'd have had a heck of a time explaining it to the kids at school.

And that was it.

A few seconds later they were gone.

I stood there in the woods just a little longer, staring at the spot in the sky where they had zoomed off into space. Then I ran as fast as I could to my gym class.

The rest of the day was pretty normal. Well, except that in the middle of the afternoon I realized I'd forgotten to get my locker key back from the Akiko robot. I had to go to the office and tell them I'd lost it. Which wasn't quite true, of course. But I figured if I told them that my locker key had been taken to another galaxy . . . Well, let's just say that sometimes it's better not to give too many details.

After school I went back home and did all the stuff I usually do. Hung around with my friend Melissa. Ate dinner with my parents. Sure enough, no one had even noticed I was gone. Weird. But kind of cool, actually.

I had a really wonderful dream that night. I was in a beautiful garden somewhere having tea with Ladmi. She had made some nice little cakes with silvery flakes on them, and we were drinking milky tea from delicate silver-and-turquoise cups. We were partially shaded by a circle of tall, leafy trees, and the sunlight that filtered down to us was warm and yellow. We were talking and laughing and eating . . . just really enjoying ourselves. It was such a beautiful dream I didn't want it to end.

But my eyes opened for some reason and I was suddenly wide awake at three in the morning. I have no idea why. Maybe it was jet lag, or spaceship lag, or whatever kind of lag it's supposed to be called. I got up, turned on the lights, and went over to my desk. I sat down cross-legged on the floor and pulled open the very bottom drawer, where I had put Ladmi's necklace the night before. I took it out, put it on, and stared at myself in the mirror on my bedroom door.

I sat that way for a very long time. I tried to imagine what Ladmi was doing at that moment and what her life would be like in the years to come. I pictured her married to some handsome prince on the planet Zullziban. I saw two or three pretty little children, each with identical brown-and-yellow wings, all of them riding around on Wolo's back in a sunny little courtyard somewhere.

I wondered if I'd ever see Ladmi again, if I'd ever get the chance to thank her for the gift. If I did get to

see her again, I wondered if she'd still call me Pigtails. For some reason I kind of hoped she would.

Finally I took the necklace off and put it back in the drawer. I climbed into bed, turned off the lights, and closed my eyes. It took a while, but before long I began to feel groggy enough to fall asleep again.

My crazy outer space adventures were over—for the time being, at least. Something told me, though, that I hadn't seen the last of my friends from the planet Smoo. They'd be back. I don't know how I knew that, but I knew it, I really did.

I opened my eyes one last time, smiled, and closed them again.

It was good to be home.

ABOUT THE AUTHOR AND ILLUSTRATOR

Mark Crilley was raised in Detroit, where his parents sometimes wondered if he wasn't from another planet. After graduating from Kalamazoo College in 1988, he traveled to Taiwan and Japan, where he taught English to students of all ages for nearly five years. It was during his stay in Japan in 1992 that he created the story of Akiko and her journey to the planet Smoo. First published as a comic book in 1995, the bimonthly Akiko series has since earned Crilley numerous award nominations, as well as a spot on *Entertainment Weekly*'s "It List" in 1998. Crilley lives with his wife, Miki, and their son, Matthew, just a few miles from the streets where he was raised. Visit Mark on the Web at www.markcrilley.com.